Blood Royal by Grant Allen

Charles Grant Blairfindie Allen was born on February 24th, 1848 at Alwington, near Kingston, Canada West (now part of Ontario).

Home schooled until 13 when his family moved to England, Grant was to become a highly regarded science writer who branched out to a fiction career and became enormously popular.

His work helped propel several genres of fiction and whilst his career was short it was enormously productive.

Grant's scientific background enabled him to root much of his work in a plausibility that was denied to others. He had little fear in challenging a society that treated women as second class citizens and creating best sellers from such works.

On October 25th 1899 Grant Allen died at his home in Hindhead, Haslemere, Surrey, England. He died just before finishing Hilda Wade. The novel's final episode, which he dictated to his friend, doctor and neighbour Sir Arthur Conan Doyle from his bed appeared under the appropriate title, The Episode of the Dead Man Who Spoke in 1900.

Index of Contents

I0553659

CHAPTER I - PERADVENTURE

Chiddingwick High Street is one of the quaintest and most picturesque bits of old town architecture to be found in England. Narrow at either end, it broadens suddenly near the middle, by a sweeping curve outward, just opposite the White Horse, where the weekly cattle-market is held, and where the timbered gable-ends cluster thickest round the ancient stone cross, now reduced as usual to a mere stump or relic. In addition to its High Street, Chiddingwick also possesses a Mayor, a Corporation, a town pump, an Early English church, a Baptist chapel, and abundant opportunities for alcoholic refreshment. The White Horse itself may boast, indeed, of being one of the most famous old coaching inns still remaining in our midst, in spite of railways. And by its big courtyard door, one bright morning' in early spring, Mr. Edmund Plantagenet, ever bland and self-satisfied, stood sunning his portly person, and surveying the world of the little town as it unrolled itself in changeful panorama before him.

'Who's that driving the Hector's pony, Tom?' Mr. Plantagenet asked of the hostler in a lordly voice, as a pretty girl went past in an unpretentious trap. 'She's a stranger in Chiddingwick.' For Mr. Plantagenet, as one of the oldest inhabitants, prided himself upon knowing, by sight at least, every person in the parish, from Lady Agatha herself to the workhouse children.

Tom removed the straw he was sucking from his mouth for a moment, as he answered, with the contempt of the horsy man for the inferior gentry: 'Oh, she! she ain't nobody, sir. That lot's the new governess.'

Mr. Plantagenet regarded the lady in the carriage with the passing interest which a gentleman of his distinction might naturally bestow upon so unimportant a personage. He was a plethoric man, of pompous aspect, and he plumed himself on being a connoisseur in female beauty.

'Not a bad-looking little girl, though, Tom,' he responded condescendingly, closing one eye and scanning her as one might scan a two-year-old filly. 'She holds herself well. I like to see a woman who can sit up straight in her place when she's driving.'

Mr. Plantagenet's opinion on all questions of deportment was much respected at Chiddingwick; so Tom made no reply save to chow a little further the meditative straw; while Mr. Plantagenet, having by this time sufficiently surveyed the street for all practical purposes, retired into the bar-parlour of the friendly White Horse for his regulation morning brandy-and-soda.

But the new governess, all unconscious of the comments she excited, drove placidly on to the principal bookseller and stationer's.

There were not many booksellers' shops in Chiddingwick; people in Surrey import their literature, if any, direct from London. But the one at whose door the pretty governess stopped was the best in the town, and would at least do well enough for the job she wanted. It bore, in fact, the proud legend, 'Wells's Select Library then by an obvious afterthought, in smaller letters, 'In connection with Mudie's.' An obsequious small boy rushed up, as she descended, to hold the Rector's horse, almost as in the days before compulsory education, when small hoys lurked unseen, on the look-out for stray ha'pence, at every street corner. Mary accepted his proffered aid with a sunny smile, and went into the shop carrying a paper parcel.

There was nobody in the place, however, to take her order; and Mary, who was a timid girl, not too sure of her position, stood for a moment irresolute, uncertain how to call the attention of the inmates. Just as she was on the point of giving it up as useless, and retiring discomfited, the door that led into the room behind the shop opened suddenly, and a young man entered. He seemed about nineteen, and he was tall and handsome, with deep-blue eyes, and long straggling locks of delicate yellow hair, that fell picturesquely though not affectedly about his ears and shoulders. He somehow reminded Mary of a painted window. She didn't know why, but instinctively, as he entered, she felt as if there were something medieval and romantic about the good-looking shopman. His face was almost statuesquely beautiful, a fair, frank, open face, like a bonny young sailor's, and the loose curls above were thrown lightly off the tall white forehead in a singularly graceful yet unstudied fashion. He was really quite Florentine. The head altogether was the head of a gentleman, and something more than that: it had the bold and clear-cut, fearless look about it that one seldom finds among our English population, except as the badge of rank and race in the very highest classes. Mary felt half ashamed of herself, indeed, for noting all these things immediately and instinctively about a mere ordinary shopman; for, after all, a shopman he was, and nothing more: though his head and face were the head and face of a gentleman of distinction, his dress was simply the every-day dress of his class and occupation. He was a son of the people. And as Mary was herself a daughter of the clergy, the eldest girl of a country rector, compelled by the many mouths and the narrow endowment at home to take a place as governess with a more favoured family at Chiddingwick Rectory, she knew she could have no possible right of any sort to take any personal interest in a bookseller's lad, however handsome and yellow-haired and distinguished-looking.

'I beg your pardon for not having come sooner,' the tall young man began in a very cultivated tone, which took Mary aback even more than did his singular and noteworthy appearance; 'but the fact is, you opened the door so very softly the bell didn't ring; and I didn't notice there was anybody in the shop, as I was busy cutting, till I happened to look up accidentally from my ream, and then I saw you. I hope I haven't kept you unnecessarily waiting?'

He spoke like a gentleman; and Mary observed, almost without remarking it, that he didn't call her 'miss,' though she was hardly even aware of the unusual omission, his manner and address were so perfectly those of a courteous and well bred equal. If she had fancied the customary title was left out on purpose, as a special tribute of disrespect to her position as governess, her sensitive little soul would have been deeply hurt by the slight, even from an utter stranger; but she felt instinctively the handsome young mail had no such intention. He didn't mean to be anything but perfectly polite, so she hardly even noticed the curious omission.

'Oh dear no,' she answered, in her timid little voice, unfolding her parcel as she spoke with a kind of shrinking fear that she must be hurting his feelings by treating him as a tradesman. 'I've only just come in; and I, well, I wanted to know whether you could bind this again for me? Or is it quite too old to be worth the trouble of binding?'

The young man took it from her hands, and looked at her as he took it. The book was a 'British Flora,' in two stout octavo volumes, and it had evidently seen wear and tear, for it was tattered and dog-eared. But he received it mechanically, without glancing at it for a moment. His eyes, in fact, were fixed hard on Mary's. A woman knows at once what a man is thinking, especially, of course, when it's herself he's thinking about; and Mary knew that minute the young man with the fine brow and the loose yellow hair was thinking in his own head how exceedingly pretty she was. That makes a girl blush under any circumstances, and all the more so when the man who thinks it is her social inferior. Now, when Mary blushed, she coloured up to her delicate shell-like ears, which made her look prettier and daintier and more charming than ever; and the young man, withdrawing his eyes guiltily and suddenly, for he, too, knew what that blush must mean, was still further confirmed in his first opinion that she was very pretty.

The young lady, however, was ashamed he should even look at her. He was accustomed to that, and yet somehow in this case it particularly hurt him. He didn't know why, but he wanted her to like him. He look up the book to cover his confusion, and examined it carefully. 'At the time of the French Revolution,' he observed, as if to himself, in a curious, far-away tone, like one who volunteers for no particular reason a piece of general information, 'many of the refugees who came to this country were compelled to take up mechanical work of the commonest description. A Rochefoucauld mended shoes, and Talleyrand was a bookbinder.'

He said it exactly as if it was a casual remark about the volume he was holding, or the comparative merits of cloth and leather, with his eyes intently fixed on the backs of the covers, and his mind to all appearance profoundly absorbed in the alternative contemplation of morocco or russia. Mary thought him the oddest young man she had ever met in her life; she fancied he must be mad, and wondered by what chance of fate or fortune he could ever have wandered into a bookseller's shop at Chiddingwick.

The young man volunteered no more stray remarks about the French Revolution, however, but continued to inspect the backs of the books with more business-like consideration. Then he turned to her quietly: 'We could do this for you very cheap in half-calf,' he said, holding it up. 'It's not at all past mending. I see it's a favourite volume; and a book of reference of the sort you're constantly using in the open air ought to have sound, stout edges. The original binding, which was cloth, is quite unsuitable, of course, for such a purpose. If you'll leave it to me, I'll do my best to make a workman-like job of it.'

There was something in the earnest way the young man spoke that made Mary feel he took a pride in his work, simple and ordinary as it was; and his instant recognition of the needs and object of the particular volume in question, which in point of fact had been her companion in many country rambles over hill or moor, seemed to her singularly different from the perfunctory habit of most common English workmen. To them, a book is just a book to be covered. She conceived in her own mind, therefore, a vague respect at once for the young man's character. But he himself was just then looking down at the volume once more, engaged in examining the inside of the binding. As he turned to the fly-leaf he gave a sudden little start of intense surprise. 'Tudor!' he murmured—'Mary Tudor! How very curious! Did this book, then, once belong to someone named Mary Tudor?'

'It belongs to me, and that's my name,' Mary answered, a little astonished, for he was gazing fixedly at her autograph on the blank page of the first volume. Never before in her experience had any shop people anywhere showed the slightest symptom of surprise at recognition of her royal surname.

The young man made a sudden gesture of curious incredulity. 'I beg your pardon,' he said, jotting down something in pencil in the inside of the book; 'do I understand you to mean your own real name is Mary Tudor?'

'Why, yes, certainly,' Mary answered, much amused at his earnestness. 'That's my own real name—Mary Empson Tudor.'

He looked at it again. 'What a singular coincidence!' he murmured to himself half inaudibly.

'It's not an uncommon name in Wales,' Mary answered, just to cover the awkwardness, for she was surprised the young man should feel any interest at all in so abstract a subject.

'Oh, that's not it,' the yellow-haired lad replied in a hasty little way. 'The coincidence is—that my name happens to be Richard Plantagenet.'

As he spoke, he drew himself up, and met her gaze once more with conscious pride in his clear blue eye. For a moment their glances answered each other; then both dropped their lids together. But Richard Plantagenet's cheek had flushed crimson meanwhile, as a very fair man's often will, almost like a girl's, and a strange fluttering had seized upon his heart well-nigh before he knew it. This was not remarkable. Mary Tudor was an extremely pretty girl; and her name seemed fateful; but who was she? Who could she be? Why had she happened to come there? Richard Plantagenet determined in his own heart that moment he would surely search this out, and never rest until he had discovered the secret of their encounter.

'You shall have it on Wednesday,' he said, coming back to the book with a sudden drop from cloudland. 'Where may I send it?' This last in the common tone of business.

'To the Rectory,' Mary answered, 'addressed to Miss Tudor.' And then Richard knew at once she must be the new governess. His eye wandered to the door. He hadn't noticed till that minute the Rectory pony; but once he saw it, he understood all; for Chiddingwick was one of those very small places where everyone knows everyone else's business. And Fraulein had gone back just three weeks ago to Hanover.

There was a moment's pause: then Mary said 'Good-morning,' sidling off a little awkwardly; for she thought Richard Plantagenet's manner a trifle embarrassing for a man in his position; and she didn't even feel quite sure he wasn't going to claim relationship with her on the strength of his surname. Now, a shopman may be handsome and gentlemanly, and a descendant of kings, but he mustn't aspire to acquaintance on such grounds as these with the family of a clergyman of the Church of England.

'Good-morning,' Richard replied with a courtly bow, like a gentleman of the old school, which indeed he was. 'Your books shall be covered as well as we can do them.'

Mary returned to the pony, and Richard to his ream, which he was cutting into sermon-paper. But Mary Tudor's pretty face seemed to haunt him at his work; and he thought to himself more than once, between the clips of the knife, that if ever he married at all, that was just the sort of girl a descendant of the Plantagenets would like to marry. Yet the last time one of his house had espoused a Tudor, he said to himself very gravely, the relative roles of man and woman were reversed; for the Tudor was Henry of Richmond, 'called Henry VII., of our younger branch and the Plantagenet was Elizabeth of York, his consort. And that was how 'the estates' went out of the family.

But 'the estates' were England, Wales, and Ireland, he often complained in the bosom of the family.

CHAPTER II - THE HEAD OF THE HOUSE

Mr. Edmund Plantagenet residence in Chiddingwick High Street was less amply commodious, he often complained in the bosom of the family, than his ancestral home at Windsor Castle, erected by his august and famous predecessor, King Edward III. of illustrious memory. Windsor Castle is a house fit for a gentleman to live in. But as Mr. Plantagenet himself had never inhabited the home of his forefathers, owing to family differences which left it for the time being in the occupation of a Lady 'belonging to the younger branch of the house', he felt the loss of his hereditary domains less keenly than might perhaps have been expected from so sensitive a person. Still, the cottage at Chiddingwick, judged even by the less exalted standard of Mr. Plantagenet's own early recollections, was by no means unduly luxuriant. For Edmund Plantagenet had been well brought up, and received in his day the education of a gentleman. Even now, in his dishonoured and neglected old age, abundant traces of the Charterhouse still remained to the bitter end in his voice and manner. But little else was left. The White Horse had stolen away whatever other relics of gentility Mr.

Plantagenet possessed, and had reduced him in his latter days to the miserable ruin of what was once a man, and even a man of letters.

It was a sad history, and, alas! a very common one. Thirty years before, when Edmund Plantagenet, not yet a believer in his own real or pretended royal descent, went up to London from Yorkshire to seek his fortune in literature, he was one of the handsomest and most popular young men in his own society. His name alone succeeded in attracting attention; we are not all of us Plantagenets. The admirable Lady Postlethwaite, arbiter in her day of literary reputation, gave the man with the royal surname the run of her well-known salon; editors accepted readily enough his inflated prose and his affected poetry; and all the world went well with him for a time, while he remained a bachelor. But one fine day Edmund Plantagenet took it into his head, like many better men, to fall in love, we have done it ourselves, and we know how catching it is, and not only to fall in love, but also, which is worse, to give effect to his feelings by actually getting married. In after-life Mr. Plantagenet regarded that unfortunate step as the one fatal error in an otherwise blameless career. He felt that with a name and prospects like his he ought at least to have married rank, title, or money. Instead of which he just threw himself away: he married only beauty, common-sense, and goodness. The first of these fades, the second palls, and the third Mr. Plantagenet was never constructed to appreciate. But rank and money appeal to all, and persist unchanged after such skin-deep attractions as intellect or good looks have ceased to interest.

From the day of his marriage, then, Edmund Plantagenet's downward career began. As a married man, he became at once of less importance in Lady Postlethwaite's society, he was so useful for dances. Editors found out by degrees that he had only affectation and audacity in place of genius; work fell short as children increased; and evil days began to close in upon the growing family. But what was worst of all, as money grew scarcer, a larger and larger proportion of it went each day to swell the receipts, at first of his club, and afterwards, when clubs became things of the past, of the nearest public-house. To make a long story short, before many years were over, Edmund Plantagenet, the young, the handsome, the promising, had degenerated from a dashing and well-bred fellow into a miserable sot of the sorriest description.

But just in proportion as his real position grew worse and worse did Mr. Plantagenet buoy himself up in secret with magnificent ideas about his origin and ancestry. Even in his best days, indeed, he would never consent to write under his own real name; he wouldn't draggle the honour of the Plantagenets in the dirt of the street, he said with fine contempt; so he adopted for literary purposes the high-sounding pseudonym of Barry Neville. But after he began to decline, and to give way to drink, his pretensions to royal blood became well-nigh ridiculous. Not, indeed, that anyone ever heard him boast noisily of his origin; Edmund Plantagenet was too clever a man of the world to adopt such futile and obvious tactics; he knew a plan worth two of that; he posed as a genuine descendant of the old Kings of England, more by tacit assumption than by open assertion. Silence played his game far better than speech. When people tried to question him on the delicate point of his pedigree, he evaded them neatly, but with a mysterious air which seemed to say every bit as plain as words could say it: 'I choose to waive my legitimate claim, and I won't allow any man to bully me into asserting it.' As he often implied to his familiar friends, he was too much a gentleman to dispute the possession of the throne with a lady.

But Mr. Plantagenet's present ostensible means of gaining an honest livelihood was by no means a regal one. He kept, as he was wont to phrase it gently himself, a temple of Terpsichore. In other words, he taught the local dancing-class. In his best days in London, when fortune still smiled upon him, he had been famed as the most graceful waltzer in Lady Postlethwaite's set; and now that the jade had deserted him, at his lowest depth, he had finally settled down as the Chiddingwick dancing-master. Sot as he was, all Chiddingwick supported him loyally, for his name's sake; even Lady

Agatha's children attended his lessons. It was a poor sort of trade, indeed, for the last of the Plantagenets; but he consoled himself under the disgrace with the cheerful reflection that he served, after all, as it were, as his own Lord Chamberlain.

On this particular night, however, of all the year, Mr. Plantagenet felt more profoundly out of humour with the world in general and his own ancestral realm of England in particular, than was at all usual with him. The fact was, his potential subjects had been treating him with marked want of consideration for his real position. Kings in exile are exposed to intolerable affronts. The landlord of the White Horse had hinted at the desirability of arrears of pay on the score of past brandies and sodas innumerable. The landlord was friendly, and proud of his guest, who 'kept the house together'; but at times he broke out in little fits of petulance. Now, Mr. Planta-genet, as it happened, had not the wherewithal to settle this little account off-hand, and he took it ill of Barnes, who, as he justly remarked, 'had had so much out of him,' that he should endeavour to hurry a gentleman of birth in the matter of payment. He sat by his own fireside, therefore, in no very amiable humour, and watched the mother bustling about the room with her domestic preparations for the family supper.

'Clarence,' Mr. Plantagenet said, after a moment of silence, to one of the younger boys, 'have you prepared your Thucydides? It's getting very late. You seem to me to be loafing about doing nothing.'

'Oh, I know it pretty well,' Clarence answered with a nonchalant air, still whittling at a bit of stick he was engaged in transforming into a homemade whistle. 'I looked it over in class. It's not very hard. Thucydides is rot—most awful rot! It won't take five minutes.'

Mr. Plantagenet, with plump fingers, rolled himself another cigarette. He had come down in the world, and left cigars far behind, a fragrant memory of the distant past; but as a gentleman he could never descend to the level of a common clay pipe.

'Very well,' he said blandly, leaning back in his chair and beaming upon Clarence: a peculiar blandness of tone and manner formed Mr. Plantagenet's keynote. 'That may do for me, perhaps; but it won't do for Richard.'

After which frank admission of his own utter abdication of parental prerogatives in favour of his own son, he proceeded very deliberately to light his cigarette and stare with placid eyes at the dilatory Clarence.

There was a minute's pause; then Mr. Plantagenet began again.

'Eleanor,' he remarked, in the same soft, self-indulgent voice, to his youngest daughter, 'you don't seem to be doing anything. I'm sure you've got some lessons to prepare for to-morrow.'

Not that Mr. Plantagenet was in the least concerned for the progress of his children's education; but the deeper they were engaged with their books, the less noise did they make with their ceaseless chatter in the one family sitting-room, and the more did they leave their fond father in peace to his own reflections.

'Oh, there's plenty of time,' Eleanor answered, with a little toss of her pretty head. 'I can do 'em by-and-by—after Dick comes in. He'll soon be coming.'

'I wish to goodness he'd come, then!' the head of the house ejaculated fervently; 'for the noise you all make when he isn't here to look after you is enough to distract a saint. All day long I have to scrape at my fiddle; and when I come back home at night I have to sit, as best I can, in a perfect bedlam. It's too much for my poor nerves. They never were vigorous. Henry, my boy, will you stop that intolerable noise?—A Jew's harp, too! Goodness gracious! what a vulgar instrument! Dick's late to-night. I wonder what keeps him.'

It was part and parcel of Mr. Plantagenet's silent method of claiming royal descent that he called all his children with studious care after the earlier Plantagenets, his real or supposed ancestors, who were Kings of England. Thus his firstborn was Richard, in memory of their distinguished predecessor, the mighty Cœur-de-Lion; his next was Lionel Clarence, after the second son of Edward IV., the particular prince upon whom Mr. Plantagenet chose to affiliate his family pedigree; and his third was Henry, that being the Plantagenet name which sat first and oftenest upon the throne of England. His eldest girl, in like manner, was christened Maud, after the foundress of his house, who married Geoffrey Plantagenet, and so introduced the blood of the Conqueror into the Angevin race; his youngest was Eleanor, after the wife of Henry II., 'who brought us Poitou and Aquitaine as heirlooms.'

Mr. Plantagenet, indeed, never overtly mentioned these interesting little points in public himself; but they oozed out, for all that, by lateral leakage, and redounded thereby much the more to their contriver's credit. His very reticence told not a little in his favour. For a dancing-master to claim by word or deed that he is de jure King of England would be to lay himself open to unsparing ridicule; but to let it be felt or inferred that he is so, without ever for one moment arrogating to himself the faintest claim to the dignity, is to pose in silence as an injured innocent, a person of most distinguished and exalted origin, with just that little suspicion of pathos and mystery about his unspoken right which makes the thing really dignified and interesting. So people at the White Horse were wont to whisper to one another in an awe-struck undertone that 'if every man had his rights, there's some as says our Mr. Plantagenet ought to be so pretty high well up where the Queen's a-sitting.' And though Mr. Plantagenet himself used gently to brush aside the flattering impeachment with one wave of his pompous hand—'All that's been altered long ago, my dear sir, by the Act of Settlement'—yet he came in for a good many stray glasses of sherry at other people's expense, on the strength of the popular belief that he might, under happier auspices, have filled a throne, instead of occupying the chair of honour by the old oak chimney-piece in a public-house parlour.

Hardly, however, had Mr. Plantagenet uttered those memorable words, 'Dick's late to-night; I wonder what keeps him,' when the front door opened, and the Heir Apparent entered.

Immediately some strange change seemed to pass by magic over the assembled household. Everybody looked up, as though an event had occurred. Mrs. Plantagenet herself, a weary-looking woman with gentle goodness beaming out of every line in her worn face, gave a sigh of relief.

'Oh, Dick,' she cried, 'I'm so glad you've come! We've all been waiting for you.'

Richard glanced round the room with a slight air of satisfaction. It was always a pleasure to him to find his father at home, and not, as was his wont, in the White Horse parlour; though, to say the truth, the only reason for Mr. Plantagenet's absence that night from his accustomed haunt was this little tiff with the landlord over his vulgar hints of payment. Then he stooped down and kissed his mother tenderly on the forehead, patted Eleanor's curly head with a brotherly caress, gave a kindly glance at Prince Hal, as he loved to call him mentally, and sat down in the easy-chair his mother pushed towards him.

For a moment there was silence; then Dick began in an explanatory voice:

'I'm sorry I'm late; but I had a piece of work to finish to-night, mother—rather particular work, too: a little bit of bookbinding.'

'You get paid extra for that, Richard, don't you?' his father asked, growing interested.

'Well, yes,' Dick answered, rather grudgingly;

'I get paid extra for that; I do it in overtime.

But that wasn't all,' he went on hurriedly, well aware that his father was debating in his own mind whether he couldn't on the strength of it borrow a shilling. 'It was a special piece of work for the new governess at the Rectory. And, mother, isn't it odd? her name's Mary Tudor!'

'There isn't much in that,' his father answered, balancing his cigarette daintily between his first and second finger. '"A' Stuarts are na sib to the King," you know, Richard. The Plantagenets who left the money had nothing to do with the Royal Family—that is to say, with us,' Mr. Plantagenet went on, catching himself up by an after-thought.

'They were mere Sheffield cutlers, people of no antecedents, who happened to take our name upon themselves by a pure flight of fancy, because they thought it high-sounding. Which it is, undoubtedly. And as for Tudors, bless your heart, they're common enough in Wales. In point of fact, though I'm proud of Elizabeth, as a by-blow of the family, we must always bear in mind that for us, my dear boy, the Tudors were never anything but a distinct mesalliance.'

'Of course,' Richard answered with profound conviction.

His father glanced at him sharply. To Mr. Plantagenet himself this shadowy claim to royal descent was a pretty toy to be employed for the mystification of strangers and the aggrandisement of the family, a lever to work on Lady Agatha's feelings; but to his eldest son it was an article of faith, a matter of the most cherished and the profoundest belief, a reason for behaving one's self in every position in life so as not to bring disgrace on so distinguished an ancestry.

A moment's silence intervened; then Dick turned round with his grave smile to Clarence:

'And how does Thucydides get on?' he asked with brotherly solicitude.

Clarence wriggled a little uneasily on his wooden chair.

'Well, it's not a hard bit,' he answered, with a shamefaced air. 'I thought I could do it in a jiffy after you came home, Dick. It won't take two minutes. It's just that piece, don't you know, about the revolt in Corcyra.'

Dick looked down at him reproachfully..

'Oh, Clarry,' he cried with a pained face, 'you know you can't have looked at it. Not a hard bit, indeed! why, it's one of the obscurest and most debated passages in all Thucydides! Now, what's the use of my getting you a nomination, old man, and coaching you so hard, and helping to pay your way at the grammar school, in hopes of your getting an Exhibition in time, if you won't work for yourself, and lift yourself on to a better position?' And he glanced at the wooden mantelpiece, on whose vacant scroll he had carved deep with his penknife his own motto in life, 'Noblesse oblige,' in Lombardic letters, for his brother's benefit.

Clarence dropped his eyes and looked really penitent.

'Well, but I say, Dick,' he answered quickly, 'if it's so awfully difficult, don't you think it 'ud be better for me to go over it with you first, just a running construe, and then I'd get a clearer idea of what the chap was driving at from the very beginning?'

'Certainly not,' Dick answered gravely, with a little concern in his voice, for he saw in this clever plea somewhat too strong an echo of Mr. Plantagenet's own fatal plausibility. 'You should spell it out first as well as you can by yourself; and then, when you've made out all you're able to with grammar and dictionary, you should come to me in the last resort to help you. Now sit down to it, there's a good boy. I shan't be able in future to help you quite as much in your work as I've been used to do.'

He spoke with a seriousness that was above his years. To say the truth, Mr. Plantagenet's habits had almost reversed their relative places in the family. Dick was naturally conscientious, having fortunately inherited his moral characteristics rather from his mother's side than from his father's; and being thrown early into the position of assistant bread-winner and chief adviser to the family, he had grown grave before his time, and felt the weight of domestic cares already heavy upon his shoulders. As for Clarence, who had answered his father with scant respect, he never thought for a moment of disobeying the wishes of his elder brother. He took up the dog-eared Thucydides that had served them both in turn, and the old Liddell and Scott that was still common property, and began conning over the chapter set before him with conspicuous diligence. Dick looked on meanwhile with no little satisfaction, while Eleanor went on with her work, in her chair in the corner, vaguely conscious all the time of meriting his approbation.

At last, just as they sat down to their frugal supper of bread and cheese and water, for by Dick's desire they were all, save one, teetotalers, Dick sprang a mine upon the assembled company by saying out all at once in a most matter-of-fact voice to his neighbour Clarry:

'No, I shan't be able to help you very much in future, I'm afraid, because, next week, I'm going up to Oxford, to try for a scholarship.'

A profound spell of awed silence followed this abrupt disclosure of a long-formed plan. Mr. Plantagenet himself was the first to break it. He rose to the occasion.

'Well, I'm glad at least, my son,' he said, in his most grandiose manner, 'you propose to give yourself the education of a gentleman.'

'And therefore,' Dick continued, with a side-glance at Clarence, 'I shall need all my spare time for my own preparation.'

CHAPTER III - DISCOUNTING IT

Mrs. Plantagenet looked across the table at her son with vague eyes of misgiving. 'This is all very sudden, Dick,' she faltered out, not without some slight tremor.

'Sudden for you, dear mother,' Dick answered, taking her hand in his own; 'but not for me.

Very much otherwise.. I've had it in my mind for a great many months; and this is what decided me.'

He drew from his pocket as he spoke a small scrap of newspaper and handed it across to her. It was a cutting from the Times. Mrs. Plantagenet read it through with swimming eyes. 'University Intelligence: Oxford. Four Foundation Scholarships will be awarded after public examination at Durham College on May 20th. Two will be of the annual value of One Hundred Pounds, for Classics; one of the same value for Natural Science; and one for Modern History. Application to be made, on or before Wednesday, the 19th, to the Rev. the Dean, at Durham College, who will also supply all needful information to intending candidates.'

The words swam in a mist before Mrs. Plantagenet's eyes. 'What does it all mean, dear Dick?' she inquired almost tearfully.

'It means, mother,' Dick answered with the gentlest tenderness, 'that Durham is the only college in the University which gives as good a Scholarship as a hundred a year for Modern History. Now, ever since I left the grammar school, I haven't had it out of my mind for a day to go, if I could, to Oxford. I think it's incumbent upon a man in my position to give himself, if possible, a University training.'

He said the words without the slightest air of conceit or swagger, but with a profound consciousness of their import; for to Richard Plantagenet the myth or legend of the ancient greatness of his family was a spur urging him ever on to make himself worthy of so glorious an ancestry. 'So I've been working and saving ever since,' he went on, 'with that idea constantly before me; and I've looked out for twelve months or more in the Times every day for the announcement of an exam, for the Durham Scholarship.'

'But you won't get it, my boy,' Mr. Plantagenet put in philosophically, after a moment's consideration. 'You never can get it. Your early disadvantages, you know, your inadequate schooling, so many young fellows well coached from Eton and Harrow!'

'If it had been a classical one, I should agree with you: I couldn't, I'm afraid,' Richard responded frankly, for he was by no means given to over-estimate his own abilities; 'but in history it's different. You see, so much of it's just our own family pedigree and details of our ancestry. That acted as a fillip, gave me an interest in the subject from the very first; and as soon as I determined to begin reading for Oxford, I felt at once my best chance would lie in Modern History. And that's why I've been working away at it as hard as ever I could in all my spare time for more than a twelvemonth.'

'But have you been reading the right books, Dick?—that's the question,' his father put in dubiously, with a critical air, making a manful effort to recall the names of the works that were most authoritative in the subject when he himself last looked at a history: 'Sharon Turner, Kemble, Palgrave, Thierry, Guizot and so forth?'

Richard had too deep a respect for the chief of the Plantagenets, miserable sot though he was, to be betrayed into a smile by this belated catalogue. He only answered with perfect gravity: 'I'm afraid none of those would be of much use to me nowadays in a Scholarship exam.: another generation has arisen, which knows not Joseph. But I've got up all the books recommended in the circular of the Board of Studies—Freeman, you know, and Stubbs and Green, and Froude and Gardner. And I've worked especially at the reigns of the earlier Plantagenets, and the development of the towns and guilds, and all that sort of thing, in Brentano and Seebohm.'

Mr. Plantagenet held his peace and looked profoundly wise. He had barely heard the names of any of these gentlemen himself: at the best of times his knowledge had always been shallow, rather showy than exact; a journalist's stock-in-trade, and since his final collapse into the ignominious position of dancing-master at Chiddingwick he had ceased to trouble himself much about any form of literature save the current newspaper. A volume of 'Barry Neville's Collected Essays,' bound in the antiquated style of the 'Book of Beauty,' with a portrait of the author in a blue frock-coat and stock for frontispiece, stood on his shelf by way of fossil evidence to his extinct literary pretensions; but Barry Neville himself had dropped with time into the usual listless apathy of a small English country town. So he held his peace, not to display his ignorance further; for he felt at once, from this glib list of authorities, that Dick's fluent display of acquaintance with so many new writers, whose very names he had never before heard, though they were well enough known in the modern world of letters to be recommended by an Oxford Board of Studies, put him hopelessly out of court on the subject under discussion.

'Jones tertius has a brother at Oxford,' Clarence put in very eagerly; 'and he's a howling swell, he lives in a room that's panelled with oak from top to bottom.'

'And if you get the Scholarship, Dick,' his mother went on wistfully, 'will you have to go and live there, and be away from us always?'

'Only half the year, mother dear,' Richard answered coaxingly; for he knew what she was thinking, how hard it would be for her to be left alone in Chiddingwick, among all those unruly children and her drunken husband, without the aid of her one help and mainstay. 'You know, there's only about five months of term, and all the rest's vacation. In vacation I'd come home, and do something to earn money towards making up the deficit.'

'It's a very long time, though, five months,' Mrs. Plantagenet said pensively. 'But, there!' she added, after a pause, brightening up, 'perhaps you won't get it.'

Grave as he usually was, Richard couldn't help bursting into a merry laugh at this queer little bit of topsy-turvy self-comfort. 'Oh, I hope to goodness I shall,' he cried, with a twinkle, 'in spite of that, mother. It won't be five months all in a lump, you know; I shall go up for some six or eight weeks at a time, never more than eight together, I believe, and then come down again. But you really needn't take it to heart just yet, for we're counting our chickens before they're hatched, after all. I mayn't get it, as you say; and, indeed, as father said just now, when one comes to think how many fellows will be in for it who have been thoroughly coached and crammed at the great public schools, my chance can't be worth much—though I mean to try it.'

Just at that moment, as Dick leaned back and looked round, the door opened, and Maud, the eldest sister, entered.

She had come home from her singing lesson; for Maud was musical, and went out as daily governess to the local tradesmen's families. She was the member of the household who most of all shared Dick's confidence. As she entered Harry looked up at her, full of conscious importance and a mouthful of Dutch cheese.

'Have you heard the news, Maudie?' he asked all breathless. 'Isn't it just ripping? Dick's going up to Oxford.'

Maud was pale and tired from a long day's work—the thankless work of teaching; but her weary face flushed red none the less at this exciting announcement, though she darted a warning look under her hat towards Richard, as much as to say:

'How could you ever have told him?'

But all she said openly was:

'Then the advertisement's come of the Durham Scholarship?'

'Yes, the advertisement's come,' Dick answered, flushing in turn. 'I got it this morning, and I'm to go up on Wednesday.'

The boys were rather disappointed at this tame announcement. It was clear Maud knew all about the great scheme already. And, indeed, she and Dick had talked it over by themselves many an evening on the hills, and debated the pros and cons of that important new departure.

Maud's face grew paler again after a minute, and she murmured half regretfully, as she unfastened her hat:

'I shall miss you if you get it, Dick. It'll be hard to do without you.'

'But it's the right thing for me to do,' Richard put in almost anxiously.

Maud spoke without the faintest hesitation' in her voice.

'Oh yes; it's the right thing,' she answered. 'Not a doubt in the world about that. It's a duty you owe to yourself, and to us—and to England. Only, of course, we shall all feel your absence a very great deal. Dick, Dick, you're so much to us! And I don't know,' she went on, as she glanced at the little ones with an uncertain air—'I don't know that I'd have mentioned it before babes and sucklings—well, till I was sure I'd got it.'

She said it with an awkward flush; for Dick caught her eye as she spoke, and read her inner meaning. She wondered he had blurted it out prematurely before her father. And Dick, too, saw his mistake. Mr. Plantagenet, big with such important news, would spread it abroad among his cronies in the White Horse parlour before tomorrow was over!

Richard turned to the children.

'Now, look here, boys,' he said gravely: 'this is a private affair, and we've talked it over here without reserve in the bosom of the family. But we've talked it over in confidence. It mustn't be repeated. If I were to go up and try for this Scholarship, and then not get it, all Chiddingwick would laugh at me for a fellow that didn't know his proper place, and had to be taught to know it.

For the honour of the family, boys, and you too, Nellie, I hope you won't whisper a word of all this to anybody in town. Consider what a disgrace it would be if I came back unsuccessful, and everybody in the parish came up and commiserated me: "We're so sorry, Mr. Dick, you failed at Oxford. But there, you see, you had such great disadvantages!"'

His handsome face burned bright red at the bare thought of such a disgrace; and the little ones, who, after all, were Plantagenets at heart as much as himself, every one of them made answer with one accord:

'We won't say a word about it.'

They promised it so earnestly, and with such perfect assurance, that Dick felt he could trust them. His eye caught Maud's. The same thought passed instinctively through both their minds. What a painful idea that the one person they couldn't beg for very shame to hold his tongue was the member of the family most likely to blab it out to the first chance comer!

Maud sat down and ate her supper. She was a pretty girl, very slender and delicate, with a fair pink-and-white skin, and curious flashing eyes, most unusual in a blonde, though she was perhaps just a shade less handsome and distinguished-looking than the Heir Apparent.

All through the meal little else was talked of than this projected revolution, Dick's great undertaking. The boys were most full of it. 'Our Dick at Oxford! It was ripping, simply ripping! A lark of the first dimensions!' Clarence made up his mind at once to go up and see Dick his very first term, in oak-panelled rooms at Durham College. They must be oak-panelled. While Harry, who had feasted on 'Verdant Green' for weeks, was anxious to know what sort of gown he'd have to wear, and whether he thought he'd have ample opportunities for fighting the proctors.

'T was a foregone conclusion. So innocently did they all discount 'Our Dick's' success, and so firmly did they believe that whatever he attempted he was certain to succeed in!

After supper Mr. Plantagenet rose with an important air, and unhooked his hat very deliberately from its peg. His wife and Dick and Maud all cried out with one voice:

'Why, surely you're not going out to-night, father!'

For to go out, they knew well, in Mr. Plantagenet's dialect, meant to spend the evening in the White Horse parlour.

'Yes, my dear,' Mr. Plantagenet answered, in his blandest tone, turning round to his wife with apologetic suavity. 'The fact is, I have a very particular engagement this evening. No, no, Dick, my boy; don't try to detain me. Gentlemen are waiting for me. The claims of social life, my dear son, so much engaged, my sole time for the world, my one hour of recreation! Besides, strangers have been specially invited to meet me—people who have heard of my literary reputation! 'T would be churlish to disappoint them.'

And, brushing his son aside, Mr. Plantagenet stuck his hat on jauntily just a trifle askew, with ponderous airiness, and strolled down the steps as he adjusted his Inverness cape on his ample shoulders, with the air of a gentleman seeking his club, with his martial cloak around him.

For in point of fact it had occurred to Mr. Plantagenet as they sat at supper that, if he burst in upon the White Horse as the first bearer of such novel and important gossip, how his son Richard was shortly going to enter as an undergraduate at Durham College, Oxford, not only would he gain for himself great honour and glory, but also some sympathizing friend, proud to possess the privilege of acquaintance with so distinguished a family, would doubtless mark his sense of the dignity of the occasion by offering its head the trifling hospitality of a brandy-and-soda. And since brandy-and-soda formed the mainspring of Mr. Plantagenet's scheme of being, so noble an opportunity for fulfilling the end and aim of his existence, he felt sure, was not to be lightly neglected.

He strolled out, all smiles, apologetic, but peremptory. As soon as he was gone, the three remaining elders glanced hard at one another with blank surmise in their eyes; but they said nothing openly. Only, in his heart, Richard blamed himself with bitter blame for his unwonted indiscretion in blurting out the whole truth. He knew that by ten to-morrow morning all the world of Chiddingwick would have heard of his projected little trip to Oxford.

When the younger ones were gone to bed, the three still held their peace and only looked at each other. Mutual shame prevented them from ever outwardly commenting on the father's weaknesses. Maud was the first to break the long deep silence.

'After this, Dick,' she said decisively, 'there's no other way out of it. You've burnt your boats. If you kill yourself to do it, you must win that Scholarship!'

'I must,' Dick answered firmly. 'And what's more, I will. I'll get it or die for it. I could never stand the disgrace, now, of coming back empty-handed to Chiddingwick without it.'

'Perhaps,' Mrs. Plantagenet suggested, speaking boldly out the thought that lurked in all their minds, 'he won't say a word of it.'

Maud and Dick looked up at her with incredulous amazement. 'Oh, mother!' was all they could say. They knew their father's moods too well by far to buoy themselves up with such impossible expectations.

'Well, it seals the business, anyhow,' Dick went on, after a moment's pause. 'I must get it now, that's simply certain. Though, to be sure, I don't know that anything could make me try much harder than I'd have tried before, for your sake, mother, and for Maud's, and the children's, and the honour of the family.'

'I wish I had your faith, Dick, in the honour of the family,' Mrs. Plantagenet sighed wearily. 'I can't feel it myself. I never could feel it, somehow. Though, of course, it's a good thing if it makes you work and hold your head up in life, and do the best you ever can for Maud and the children. Anything's good that's an incentive to exertion. Yet I often wish, when I see how hard you both have to toil and moil, with the music and all that, we didn't belong to the royal stock at all, but to the other Plantagenets, who left the money.'

Both Richard and Maud exclaimed with one accord at these painful words: 'Oh, don't, dear mother!' To them, her speech sounded like sheer desecration. Faith in their own unsullied Plantagenet blood was for both a religion. And, indeed, no wonder. It had spurred them on to all that was highest and best within them. To give up that magnificent heritage of princely descent for mere filthy lucre would have seemed to either an unspeakable degradation. They loved their mother dearly; yet they often reflected, in a vague, half-unconscious sort of undercurrent of thought, that after all she was not herself a born Plantagenet, as they were; she had only married into the family, and couldn't be expected to feel quite as they did on so domestic a matter. It never struck either of them that in point of fact all those better qualities in themselves which made them so jealous for the honour of the family had descended to them solely from their mother's side of the house, and were altogether alien to the lower nature of that good-humoured, idle, unprincipled scamp and ne'er-do-well, their father.

At the very same moment, indeed, in the cosiest corner of the White Horse parlour, Mr. Plantagenet himself, the head of the house, was observing complacently, in a mellifluous voice, to an eager little group of admiring listeners: 'Yes, gentlemen, my son Richard, I'm proud to say, will shortly begin his career at Oxford University. I'm a poor man myself, I admit; I might have been richer but for untoward events; and circumstances have compelled me to submit in my old age to a degrading profession, for which neither my birth, my education, nor my literary habits have naturally fitted me. But I trust I have, at least, been a good father to my children. A good—father—to my children. I have given them the very best education this poor town can afford; and now, though I know it will sadly cripple my slender resources, I mean to make a struggle, my friends, a manful struggle, and send my boy Richard up to Oxford. Richard has brains, undoubted brains; he's proud and reserved, as you all know, and doesn't shine in society; he lacks the proper qualities; but he has undoubted brains, for all that; and brilliancy, I know to my cost'—here he heaved a deep sigh—'is often a pitfall to a man of genius. Richard hasn't genius; but he's industrious and plodding, and possesses, I'm told, a remarkable acquaintance with the history of his country. So I've made up my mind to brave the effort and send him up to our ancestral University. He may do something in time to repair the broken fortunes of a respectable family. Gentlemen,' Mr. Plantagenet went on, glancing round him for confirmation of his coming statement, 'I think you'll all bear me witness that I've never boasted or bragged about my family in any way; but you'll all admit, too, that my family is a respectable one, and that the name I bear has not been wholly undistinguished in the history of this country. Thank you, sir; I'm very much obliged indeed to you for your kindness; I don't mind if I do. Brandy, if you please, as usual, Miss Brooks, and a split soda. Gentlemen, I thank you for your generous sympathy. Misfortune has not wholly deprived me, I'm proud to notice, of appreciative friends. I will drain this sparkling beaker, which my neighbour is good enough to offer, to an appropriate toast, the toast of Success to Richard Plantagenet of Durham College, Oxford.'

CHAPTER IV - A ROYAL POURPARLER

Next morning, when Richard went down to his work in town, Mr. Wells, his employer, accosted him at once with the unwelcome greeting:

'Hullo, Plantagenet, so I hear you're going up to college at Oxford!'

Nothing on earth could well have been more unpleasant for poor Dick. He saw at once from Mr. Wells's tone that his father must have bragged: he must have spoken of the projected trip at the White Horse last night, not as a mere speculative journey in search of a problematical and uncertain Scholarship, but as a fait accompli, a domestic arrangement dependent on the mere will of the house of Plantagenet. He must have treated his decision as when a Duke decides that he shall send his son and heir to Christ Church or Trinity.

This mode of envisaging the subject was doubly annoying to Dick, for not only would he feel most keenly the disgrace of returning empty-handed if he failed in the examination, but relations might perhaps become strained meanwhile between himself and Mr. Wells, if the employer thought he might at any moment be deprived of the assistant's services. However, we must all answer for the sins of our fathers: there was nothing for it now but to brazen it out as best he might; so Dick at once confided to his master the true state of the case, explaining that he would only want a few days' holiday, during which he engaged to supply an efficient substitute; that his going to Oxford permanently must depend on his success in the Scholarship examination; and that even if he succeeded, which he modestly judged unlikely, he wouldn't need to give up his present engagement and go into residence at the University till October.

These explanations, frankly given with manly candour, had the good effect of visibly mollifying Mr. Wells's nascent and half-spoken resentment. Richard had noticed just at first that he assumed a sarcastic and somewhat aggrieved tone, as one who might have expected to be the first person informed of this intended new departure. But as soon as all was satisfactorily cleared up, the bookseller's manner changed immediately, and he displayed instead a genuine interest in the success of the great undertaking. To say the truth, Mr. Wells was not a little proud of his unique assistant. He regarded him with respect, not unmixed with pity.

All Chiddingwick, indeed, took a certain compassionate interest in the Plantagenet family. They were, so to speak, public property and local celebrities. Lady Agatha Moore herself, the wife of the Squire, and an Earl's daughter, always asked Mrs. Plantagenet to her annual garden-party. Chiddingwickians pointed out the head of the house to strangers, and observed with pardonable possessive pride: 'That's our poor old dancing-master; he's a Plantagenet born, and some people say if it hadn't been for those unfortunate Wars of the Roses he'd have been King of England. But now he holds classes at the White Horse Assembly Rooms.'

Much more then had Mr. Wells special reason to be proud of his own personal relations with the heir of the house, the final inheritor of so much shadowy and hypothetical splendour. The moment he learned the real nature of Dick Plantagenet's errand, he was kindness itself to his clever assistant. He desired to give Dick every indulgence in his power. Mind the shop? No, certainly not! Richard would want all his time now to cram for the examination. He must cram, cram, cram; there was nothing like cramming!

Mr. Wells, laudably desirous of keeping well abreast with the educational movement of the present day, laid immense stress upon this absolute necessity for cram in the modern world. He even advised Richard to learn by heart the names and dates of all the English monarchs Dick could hardly forbear a smile at this naïve but well-meant proposal. He had worked hard at Modern History, both British and continental, in all his spare time, ever since he left the grammar school, and few men at the University knew as much as he did of our mediaeval annals. We are all for 'epochs' nowadays; and Dick's epoch was the earlier middle age of feudalism. But the notion that anything so childish as the names and dates of kings could serve his purpose tickled his gravity not a little. Still, the advice was kindly meant, up to Mr. Wells's lights, and Dick received it with grave courtesy, making answer politely that all these details were already familiar to him.

During the four days that remained before the trip to Oxford, Mr. Wells wouldn't hear of Richard's doing any more work in the shop than was absolutely necessary. He must spend all his time, the good man said, in reading Hume and Smollett, the latest historical authorities of whom the Chiddingwick bookseller had any personal knowledge. Dick availed himself for the most part of his employer's kindness; but there was one piece of work, he said, which he couldn't neglect, no matter what happened. It was a certain bookbinding job of no very great import, just a couple of volumes to cover in half-calf for the governess at the Rectory. Yet he insisted upon doing it.

Somehow, though he had only seen Mary Tudor once, for those few minutes in the shop, he attached a very singular and sentimental importance to binding that book for her. She was a pretty girl, for one thing, an extremely pretty girl, and he admired her intensely. But that wasn't all; she was a Tudor, as well, and he was a Plantagenet. In some vague, half-conscious way he reflected more than once that 'it had gone with a Tudor, and with a Tudor it might come back again.' What he meant by that it he hardly knew himself. Certainly not the crown of this United Kingdom; for Dick was far too good a student of constitutional history not to be thoroughly aware that the crown of England itself was elective, not hereditary; and he had far too much common-sense to suppose for one moment that the people of these three realms would desire to disturb the Act of Settlement and repeal the Union in order to place a local dancing-master or a bookseller's assistant on the throne of England—for to Scotland he hadn't even the shadowy claim of an outside pretender. As he put it himself, 'We were fairly beaten out of there once for all by the Bruce, and had never at the best of times any claim to speak of.' No; what he meant by It was rather some dim past greatness of the Plantagenet family, which the bookseller's lad hoped to win back to some small extent in the noblest and best of all ways—by deserving it.

The days wore away; Stubbs and Freeman were well thumbed; the two books for Mary Tudor were bound in the daintiest fashion known to Chiddingwickian art, and on the morning of the eventful Wednesday itself, when he was first to try his fate at Oxford, Dick took them up in person, neatly wrapped in white tissue-paper, to the door of the Rectory.

Half-way up the garden-path Mary met him by accident. She was walking in the grounds with one of the younger children; and Dick, whose quick imagination had built up already a curious castle in the air, felt half shocked to find that a future Queen of England, Wales, and Ireland (de jure) should be set to take care of the Rector's babies. However, he forgot his indignation when Mary, recognising him, advanced with a pleasant smile, her smile was always considered the prettiest thing about her, and said in a tone as if addressed to an equal:

'Oh, you've brought back my books, have you? That's punctuality itself. Don't mind taking them to the door. How much are they, please? I'll pay at once for them.'

Now, this was a trifle disconcerting to Dick, who had reasons of his own for not wishing her to open the parcel before him. Still, as there was no way out of it, he answered in a somewhat shamefaced and embarrassed voice: 'It comes to three-and-sixpence.'

Mary had opened the packet meanwhile, and glanced hastily at the covers. She saw in a second that the bookseller's lad had exceeded her instructions. For the books were bound in full calf, very dainty and delicate, and on the front cover of each was stamped in excellent workmanship a Tudor rose, with the initials M. T. intertwined in a neat little monogram beneath it. She looked at them for a moment with blank dismay in her eye, thinking just at first what a lot he must be going to charge her for it; then, as he named the price, a flush of shame rose of a sudden to her soft round cheek.

'Oh no,' she said hurriedly. 'It must be more than that. You couldn't possibly bind them so for only three-and-sixpence!'

'Yes, I did,' Dick answered, now as crimson as herself. 'You'll find the bill inside. Mr. Wells wrote it out. There's no error at all. You'll see it's what I tell you.'

Mary fingered her well-worn purse with uncertain fingers.

'Surely,' she said again, 'you've done it all in calf. Mr. Wells can't have known exactly how you were doing it.'

This put a Plantagenet at once upon his mettle.

'Certainly he did,' Dick answered, almost haughtily. 'It was a remnant of calf, no use for anything else, that I just made fit by designing those corners. He said I could use it up if I cared to take the trouble. And I did care to take the trouble, and to cut a block for the rose, and to put on the monogram, which was all my own business, in my own overtime. Three-and-sixpence is the amount it's entered in the books for.'

Mary gazed hard at him in doubt. She scarcely knew what to do. She felt by pure instinct he was too much of a gentleman to insult him by offering him money for what had obviously been a labour of love to him; and yet, for her own part, she didn't like to receive those handsome covers to some extent as a present from a perfect stranger, and especially from a man in his peculiar position. Still, what else could she do? The books were her own; she couldn't refuse them now, merely because he chose to put a Tudor rose upon them, all the more as they contained those little marginal notes of 'localities' and 'finds' which even the amateur botanist prizes in his heart above all printed records; and she couldn't bear to ask this grave and dignified young man to take the volumes back, remove the covers on which he had evidently spent so much pains and thought, and replace them by three-and-sixpence worth of plain cloth, unlettered. In the end she was constrained to say frigidly, in a lowered voice:

'They're extremely pretty. It was good of you to take so much trouble about an old book like this.

There's the money; thank you—and—I'm greatly obliged to you.'

The words stuck in her throat. She said them almost necessarily with some little stiffness. And as she spoke she looked down, and dug her parasol into the gravel of the path for nervousness. But Richard Plantagenet's pride was far deeper than her own. He took the money frankly; that was Mr. Wells's; then he answered in that lordly voice he had inherited from his father:

'I'm glad you like the design. It's not quite original; I copied it myself with a few variations from the cover of a book that once belonged to Margaret Tudor. Her initials and yours are the same. But I see you think I oughtn't to have done it. I'm sorry for that; yet I had some excuse. I thought a Plantagenet might venture to take a little more pains than usual over a book for a Tudor. Noblesse oblige.'

And as he spoke, standing a yard or two off her, with an air of stately dignity, he lifted his hat, and then moved slowly off down the path to the gate again.

Mary didn't know why, but with one of those impulsive fits which often come over sympathetic women, she ran hastily after him.

'I beg your pardon,' she said, catching him up, and looking into his face with her own as flushed as his. 'I'm afraid I've hurt you. I'm sure I didn't mean to. It was very, very kind of you to design and print that monogram so nicely. I understand your reasons, and I'm immensely obliged. It's a beautiful design. I shall be proud to possess it.'

As for Richard, he dared hardly raise his eyes to meet hers, they were so full of tears. This rebuff was very hard on him. But the tell-tale moisture didn't quite escape Mary.

'Thank you,' he said simply. I meant no rudeness; very much the contrary. The coincidence interested me; it made me wish to do the thing for you as well as I could. I'm sorry if I was obtrusive. But, one sometimes forgets, or perhaps remembers. It's good of you to speak so kindly.'

And he raised his hat once more, and, walking rapidly off without another word, disappeared down the road in the direction of the High Street.

As soon as he was gone Mary went back into the Rectory. Mrs. Tradescant, the Rector's wife, was standing in the hall. Mary reflected at once that the little girl had listened open-eared to all this queer colloquy, and that, to prevent misapprehension, the best thing she could do would be to report it all herself before the child could speak of it. So she told the whole story of the strange young man who had insisted on binding her poor dog-eared old botany-book in such regal fashion. Mrs. Tradescant glanced at it, and only smiled.

'Oh, my dear, you mustn't mind him,' she said. 'He's one of those crazy Plantagenets. They're a very queer lot—as mad as hatters. The poor old father's a drunken old wretch; come down in the world, they say. He teaches dancing; but his mania is that he ought by rights to be King of England. He never says so openly, you know; he's too cunning for that; but in a covert sort of way he lays tacit claim to it. The son's a very well-con-ducted young man in his own rank, I believe, but as cracked as the father; and as for the daughter, oh, my dear, such a stuck-up sort of a girl, with a feather in her hat and a bee in her bonnet, who goes out and gives music-lessons! It's dreadful, really! She plays the violin rather nicely, I hear; but she's an odious creature. The books? Oh yes, that's just the sort of thing Dick Plantagenet would love. He's mad on antiquity. If he saw on the title-page your name was Mary Tudor, he'd accept you at once as a remote cousin, and he'd claim acquaintance off-hand by a royal monogram. The rose is not bad. But the best thing you can do is to take no further notice of him.'

A little later that very same morning, however, Richard Plantagenet, mad or sane, was speeding away across country, in a parliamentary train, towards Reading and Oxford, decided in his own mind now about two separate plans he had deeply at heart. The first one was that, for the honour of the Plantagenets, he mustn't fail to get that Scholarship at Durham College; the second was that, when he came back with it to Chiddingwick, he must make Mary Tudor understand he was at least a gentleman. He was rather less in love with her, to be sure, after this second meeting, than he had been after the first; but, still, he liked her immensely, and in spite of her coldness was somehow attracted towards her; and he couldn't bear to think a mere Welsh Tudor, not even really royal, should feel herself degraded by receiving a gift of a daintily-bound book from the hands of the Heir Apparent of the true and only Plantagenets.

CHAPTER V - GOOD SOCIETY

Dick knew nothing of Oxford, and would hardly even have guessed where in the town to locate himself while the examination was going on, had not his old head-master at Chiddingwick Grammar School supplied him with the address of a small hotel, much frequented by studious and economical young men on similar errands. Hither, then, he repaired, Gladstone bag in hand, and engaged a modest second-floor room; after which, with much trepidation, he sallied forth at once in his best black suit to call in due form on the Reverend the Dean at Durham College.

By the door of the Saracen's Head, which was the old-fashioned name of his old-fashioned hostelry, two young men, mere overgrown schoolboys of the Oxford pattern, lounged, chatting and chaffing together, as if bent on some small matter of insignificant importance. Each swung a light cane, and each looked and talked as if the town were his freehold. One was a fellow in a loose gray tweed suit and a broad-brimmed slouch-hat of affectedly large and poetical pretensions; the other was a faster-looking and bolder young person, yet more quietly clad in a black cut-away coat and a billycock hat, to which commonplace afternoon costume of the English gentleman he nevertheless managed to give a touch of distinctly rowdy and rapid character.

As Dick passed them on the steps to go forth into the street, the young man in black observed oracularly: 'Lamb ten to the slaughter to which his companion answered with brisk good-humour in the self-same dialect: 'Lamb ten it is; these meadows pullulate; we shall have a full field of them.'

By a burst of inspiration Dick somehow gathered that they were referring to the field for the Durham Scholarships, and that they knew of ten candidates at least in the place who were also going in for them. He didn't much care for the looks of his two fellow-competitors, for such he judged them to be; but the mere natural loneliness of a sensitive young man in such strange conditions somehow' prompted him, almost against his will, to accost them.

'I beg your pardon,' he said timidly, in a rather soft voice, 'but I, that is to say, could you either of you tell me which is the nearest way to Durham College?'

The lad in the gray tweed suit laughed, and surveyed him from head to foot with a somewhat supercilious glance as he answered with a curious self-assertive swagger: 'You're going to call on the Dean, I suppose. Well, so are we. Durham it is. If you want to know the way, you can come along with us.'

Companionship in misery is dear to the unsophisticated human soul; and Richard, in spite of all his father's lessons in deportment, shrank so profoundly from this initial ordeal of the introductory visit that he was really grateful to the supercilious youth in the broad-brimmed hat for his condescending offer. Though, to be sure, if it came to that, nobody in England had a right to be either supercilious or condescending to a scion of the Plantagenets.

'Thank you,' he said, a little nervously. 'This is my first visit to Oxford, and I don't know my way about. But I suppose you're not in for the Scholarship yourself?' And he gazed half unconsciously at his new acquaintance's gray tweed suit and big sombrero, which were certainly somewhat noisy for a formal visit.

The young man in the billycock interpreted the glance aright, and answered it promptly.

'Oh, you don't know my friend,' he said, with a twinkle in his eye and a jerk of the head towards the lad in gray tweed; 'this is Gillingham of Rugby, otherwise known as the Born Poet. England expects every man to do his duty; but she never expects Gillingham to dress or behave like the vest of us poor common everyday mortals. And quite right, too. What's the good of being a born poet, I should like to know, if you've got to mind your P's and Q's just like other people?'

'Well, I'm certainly glad I'm not an Other Person,' Gillingham responded calmly, with a nonchalant air of acknowledged superiority.

'Other people, for the most part, are so profoundly uninteresting! But if you're going to walk with us, let me complete the introduction my friend has begun. This is Faussett of Rugby, otherwise known as the Born Philistine. Congenitally incapable of the faintest tincture of culture himself, he regards the possession of that alien attribute by others as simply ridiculous.' Gillingham waved his hand vaguely towards the horizon in general. 'Disregard what he says,' he went on, 'as unworthy a serious person's intelligent consideration, and dismiss him to that limbo where he finds himself most at home, among the rowdy mob of all the Gaths and Askelons!'

Dick hardly knew how to comport himself in such unwonted company. Gillingham's manner was unlike anything else to which he had ever been accustomed. But he felt dimly aware that politeness compelled him to give his own name in return for the others'; so he faltered out somewhat feebly, 'My name's Plantagenet,' and then relapsed into a timid silence.

'Whew! How's that for arme?' Gillingham exclaimed, taken aback. 'Rather high, Tom, isn't it? Are you any relation to the late family so called, who were Kings of England?'

This was a point-blank question which Dick could hardly avoid; but he got over the thin ice warily by answering, with a smile:

'I never heard of more than one family of Plantagenets in England.'

'Eton, of course?' Gillingham suggested with a languid look. 'It must Le Eton. It was founded by an ancestor.'

To Dick himself the question of the Plantagenet pedigree was too sacred for a jest; but he saw the only way to treat the matter in the present company was by joking; so he answered with a little laugh:

'I believe there's no provision there for the founder's kin, so I didn't benefit by it. I come only from a very small country grammar school—Chiddingwick, in Surrey.'

'Chiddingwick! Chiddingwick! Never knew there was such a place,' Gillingham put in with crushing emphasis. And he said it with an air which showed at once so insignificant a school was wholly unworthy a Born Poet's attention.

As for the Philistine, he laughed.

'Well, which are you going in for?' he asked, with a careless swing of his cane: 'The science, or the classics?'

'Neither,' Dick answered. 'My line's modern history.'

With a sudden little start, Gillingham seemed to wake up to interest. 'So's mine,' he put in, looking extremely wise. 'It's the one subject now taught at our existing Universities that a creature with a soul, immortal or otherwise, would be justified in bothering his head about for one moment. Classics and 'mathematics! oh, fiddlesticks! shade of Shelley, my gorge rises at them!'

'You won't have any chance against Gillingham, though,' Faussett interposed with profound conviction. 'He's a fearful dab at history! You never knew such a howler. He's read pretty well everything that's ever been written in it from the earliest ages to the present time. Herodotus and York Powell alike at his finger-ends! We consider at Rugby that a man's got to get up uncommon early if he wants to take a rise out of Trevor Gillingham.'

'I'm sorry for that,' Dick answered quite earnestly, astonished, now he stood face to face with these men of the world, at his own presumption in venturing even to try his luck against them. 'For I can't have many shots at Scholarships myself; and, unless I get one, I can't afford to come up at all to the University.'

His very pride made him confess this much to his new friends at once, for he didn't wish to seem as if he made their acquaintance under false pretences.

'Oh, for my part, I don't care two pence about the coin,' Gillingham replied with lordly indifference, cocking his hat yet a trifle more one-sidedly than ever. 'Only, the commoner's gown, you know, is such, an inartistic monstrosity! I couldn't bear to wear it! And if one goes to a college at all, one likes to feel one goes on the very best possible footing, as a member of the foundation, and not as a mere outsider, admitted on sufferance.'

It made poor Dick's mouth water to hear the fellow talk so. What a shame these rich men, mere nouveaux riches, too, by the side of a Plantagenet, should come in like this, and take for pure honour and glory the coveted allowance that other men need as bare provision for their career at the University! He thought it quite unjustifiable. So he walked along in silence the rest of the way to the college gate, while Gillingham and Faussett, schoolboys out of school, continued to talk and chaff and swing their cherry canes in unconcerned good-humour. It was evident the ceremony meant very little to them, which to him meant more than he cared even to acknowledge. Faussett, indeed, had no expectation of a scholarship for himself at all. He went in for it for form's sake, at his father's desire, 'just to satisfy the governor', and in hopes it might secure him an offer of rooms from the college authorities.

The first sight of the walls and outer gate of Durham impressed and overawed Dick Plantagenet not a little. To boys brought up in one of our great public schools, indeed, the aspect of Magdalen or Merton or Oriel has in it nothing of the awesome or appalling. It's only the same old familiar quads on a larger scale over again. But to lads whose whole ideas have been formed from the first at a small country grammar school, the earliest glimpse of University life is something almost terrifying. Richard looked up at the big gate, with its sculptured saints in shrine-like niches, and then beyond again at the great quadrangle with its huge chapel window and its ivy-covered hall, and wondered to himself how he could ever have dreamt of trying to force himself in among so much unwonted splendour. A few lazy undergraduates, great overgrown schoolboys, were lounging about the quad in very careless attitudes. Some were in flannels, bound for the cricket-field or the tennis-courts; others, who were boating men, stood endued in most gorgeous many-coloured blazers. Dick regarded them with awe as dreadfully grand young gentlemen, and trembled to fancy what they would say or think of his carefully-kept black coat, rather shiny at the seams, and his well-brushed hat preserved over from last season. His heart sank within him at the novelty of his surroundings. But just at that moment, in the very nick of time, he raised his eyes by accident, and caught sight, of what? Why the Plantagenet leopards, three deep, upon the façade of the gatehouse. At view of those familiar beasts, the cognisance of his ancestors, he plucked up courage again; after all, he was a Plantagenet, and a member of his own house had founded and endowed that lordly pile he half shrank from entering.

Gillingham saw where his eyes wandered, and half read his unspoken thought. 'Ah, the family arms!' he said, laughing a quick little laugh.

'You're to the manner born here. If any preference is shown to founder's kin, you ought to beat us all at this shop, Plantagenet!' And he passed under the big gateway with the lordly tread of the rich man's son, who walks this world without one pang of passing dread at that ubiquitous and unsocial British notice, 'Trespassers will be prosecuted.'

Dick followed him, trembling, into the large paved quad, and up the stone steps of the Dean's staircase, and quivered visibly to Faussett's naked eye as they were all three ushered into the great man's presence. The room was panelled, after Clarence's own heart: severe engravings from early Italian masters alone relieved the monotony of its old wooden wainscots.

A servant announced their names. The Dean, a precise-looking person in most clerical dress, sealed at a little oak table all littered with papers, turned listlessly round in his swinging chair to receive them. 'Mr. Gillingham of Rugby,' he said, focussing his eye-glass on the credentials of respectability which the Born Poet presented to him. 'Oh, yes, that's all right. Sixth Form—h'm, h'm. Your headmaster was so kind as to write to me about you. I'm very glad to see you at Barham, I'm sure, Mr. Gillingham; hope we may number you among ourselves before long. I've had the pleasure of meeting your father once—I think it was at Athens. Or no, the Piræus. Sir Bernard was good enough to use his influence in securing me an escort from the Greek Government for my explorations in Boetia. Country very much disturbed; soldiers absolutely necessary. These papers are quite satisfactory, of course; h'm, h'm! highly satisfactory. Your Head tells me you write verses, too. Well, well, we shall see. You'll go in for the Newdigate. The Keats of the future!'

'We call him the Born Poet at Rugby, sir,' Paussett put in, somewhat mischievously.

'And you're going in for the modern history examination?' the Dean said, smiling, but otherwise not heeding the cheeky interruption. 'Well, history will be flattered.' He readjusted his eyeglass. 'Mr. Faussett: Rugby, too, I believe? H'm; h'm; well, your credentials are respectable—decidedly respectable, though by no means brilliant. You've a brother at Christ Church, I understand. Ah, yes; exactly. You take up classics. Quite so. And now for you, sir. Let me see.' He dropped his eyeglass, and stared hard at the letter Richard laid before him. 'Mr.—er—Plantagenet, of—what is it?—oh, I see—Chiddingwick Grammar School. Chiddingwick, Chiddingwick? H'm? h'm? never heard of it. Eh? What's that? In Yorkshire, is it? Oh, ah, in Surrey; exactly; quite so. You're a candidate for the History Scholarship, it seems. Well, the name Plantagenet's not unknown in history. That'll do, Mr. Plantagenet; you can go. Good-morning. Examination begins in hall to-morrow at ten o'clock punctually.—Mr. Gillingham, will you and our friend lunch with me on Friday at half-past one? No engagement? Most fortunate.' And with a glance at the papers still scattered about his desk, he dismissed them silently.

Dick slunk down the steps with a more oppressive consciousness of his own utter nothingness in the scheme of things than he had ever before in his life experienced. It was impossible for him to overlook the obvious difference between the nature of the reception he had himself obtained and that held out to the son of Sir Bernard Gillingham and his companion from Rugby. He almost regretted now he had ever been rash enough to think of pitting his own home-bred culture against that of these rich men's sons, taught by first-class masters at great public schools, and learned in all the learning of the Egyptians.

As they emerged into Oriel Street, Faussett turned to him with a broad smile.

'I just cheeked him about the Born Poet, didn't I?' he said, laughing. 'But he took it like an angel. You see, they've heard a good bit about Gillingham already. That makes all the difference. Our Head backs Gillingham for next Poet Laureate, if Tennyson holds out long enough. He'll get this history thing slap off; you see if he doesn't. I could tell from the Dean's manner it was as good as decided. They mean to give it to him.'

'But, surely,' Dick cried, flushing up with honest indignation, 'they wouldn't treat it as a foregone conclusion like that. They wouldn't bring us all up here, and put us to the trouble and expense of an hotel, and make us work three days, if they didn't mean to abide by the result of the examination!'

Faussett gazed at him and smiled.

'Well, you are green!' he answered, laughing.

'You are just a verdant one! What lovely simplicity! You don't mean to say you think that's the way this world is governed? I've a father in the House, and I trust I know better. Kissing goes by favour. They'll give it to Gillingham; you may take your oath on that. And a jolly good thing, too; for I'm sure he deserves it!'

Gillingham himself was a trifle more modest and also more cautious. He made no prediction. Brought up entirely in diplomatic circles, he did credit to his teachers. He contented himself with saying in an oracular voice, 'The race is not to the swift, nor the battle to the strong,' and throwing back his head in his most poetical manner.

This was a safe quotation, for it committed him to nothing. If he won, it would pass as very charming modesty; if he lost, it would discount and condone his failure.

As for Dick, he strolled with his two chance acquaintances down the beautiful High Street and into the gardens at Magdalen, very heavy in heart at their dire predictions. The cloisters themselves failed to bring him comfort. He felt himself foredoomed already to a disastrous fiasco. So many places and things he had only read about in books, this brilliant, easy-going, very grown-up Trevor Gillingham had seen and mixed in and made himself a part of. He had pervaded the Continent.

The more Gillingham talked, indeed, the more Dick's heart sank. Why, the man knew well every historical site and building in Britain or out of it! History to him was not an old almanac, but an affair of real life. Paris, Brussels, Rome—Bath, Lincoln, Holyrood—he had known and seen them! Dick longed to go back and hide his own discomfited head once more in the congenial obscurity of dear sleepy old Chiddingwick.

But how could he ever go back without that boasted Scholarship? How cover his defeat after Mr. Plantagenet's foolish talk at the White Horse? How face his fellow-townsmen—and Mary Tudor? For very shame's sake, he felt he must brazen it out now, and do the best he knew—for the honour of the family.

CHAPTER VI - THE PROOF OF THE PUDDING

Dick slept little that night: he lay awake, despondent. Next day he rose un-refreshed, and by a quarter to ten was in the quad at Durham. Not another candidate as yet had showed up so early. But undergraduates were astir, moving aimlessly across the quad in caps and gowns, and staring hard at the intruder, as one might stare at a strange wild beast from some distant country. Dick shrank nervously from their gaze, hardly daring to remember how he had hoped at Chiddingwick to be reckoned in their number. One thing only gave him courage every time he raised his eyes, the Plantagenet leopards on the facade of the buildings. Should he, the descendant of so many great kings, ataris editas regibus, should he slink ashamed from the sons of men whom his ancestors would have treated as rebellious subjects? He refused such degradation. For the honour of the Plantagenets he would still do his best; and more than his best the Black Prince himself could never have accomplished.

He lounged around the quad till the doors of the hall were opened. A minute before that time Gillingham strolled casually up in sombrero and gray suit, and nodded a distant nod to him.

'Morning, Plantagenet,' he said languidly, putting his pipe in his pocket; and it was with an effort that Dick managed to answer, as if unconcerned: 'Good-morning, Gillingham.'

The first paper was a stiff one, a feeler on general European history, to begin with. Dick glanced over it in haste, and saw to his alarm and horror a great many questions that seemed painfully unfamiliar. Who on earth were Jacopo Nardi, and Requesens, and Jean Bey? What was meant by the publication of the Edict of Rostock? And he thought himself a historian! Pah! this was simply horrible! He glanced up mutely at the other candidates. One or two of them appeared every bit as ill at ease as himself; but others smiled satisfied; and as for the Born Poet, leaning back against the wall with pen poised in one hand, he surveyed the printed form with a pleased smirk on his face that said as plainly as words could say it, 'This paper was just made for me! If I'd chosen the questions myself, I couldn't have chosen anything that would have suited me better.' He set to work at it at once with a business-like air, while Dick chewed his quill-pen, evidently flooring every item in the lot consecutively. No picking and choosing for him; he dashed straight at it: Peter the Great or Charles XII., Cæsar Borgia or Robespierre, it was all one, Dick could see, to the Born Poet. He wrote away for dear life with equal promptitude on the Reformation in Germany and the Picts in Scotland; he seemed just as much at home with the Moors at Granada as with the Normans in Sicily; he never hesitated for a second over that fearful stumper, 'State what you know of the rise and progress of the Bavarian Monarchy'; and he splashed off three whole pages of crowded foolscap without turning a hair in answer to the command: 'Describe succinctly the alterations effected in the Polish Constitution during the seventeenth century.' Such encyclopaedic knowledge appalled and alarmed poor Dick, with his narrower British outlook. He began to feel he had been ill-advised indeed to measure his own strength against the diplomatic service and the historical geniuses of the old foundations.

When they came out at mid-day he compared notes on their respective performances with Gillingham. All three young men lunched together at the Saracen's Head, Dick ordering cold beef and a glass of water, for Mr. Plantagenet's example had made him a teetotaler; while the two Rugby boys fared sumptuously every day off cutlets, asparagus, fresh strawberries, and claret. Gillingham had walked through the paper, he averred, a set of absurdly elementary questions.

'I floored Jacopo Nardi,' he remarked with a genial smile, 'and I simply polished off the Edict of Rostock.'

Dick, more despondent, went through it in detail, confessing with shame to entire ignorance of more than one important matter.

'Oh, the Poet wins!' Faussett exclaimed, with deep admiration. 'He wins in a canter. I tell you, it's no use any other fellow going in when the Poet's in the field. It's Gillingham first, and the rest nowhere. He knows his books, you see. He's a fearful pro. at them.'

'Perhaps there's a dark horse, though,' Gillingham suggested, smiling. 'The Prince of the Blood may hold the lists, after all, against all comers.'

'Perhaps so,' Faussett answered with a short little laugh. 'But I'll back the Rugby lot against the field, all the same, for a fiver. The rest are rank outsiders. Even money on the Poet! Now, gentlemen, now's your chance! The Poet for a fiver! even money on the Poet, the Poet wins! "Who'll back the Plantagenet?"'

Dick coloured to the very roots of his hair; he felt himself beaten in the race beforehand. Oh, why had he ever come up to this glorious, impossible place at all? And why did he ever confide the secret of his intentions to the imprudent head of the house of Plantagenet?

That day and the next day it was always the same. He sat and bit his pen, and looked hard at the questions, and waited for inspiration that never seemed to come; while Gillingham, the brilliant, the omniscient, the practical, fully equipped at all points, went on and wrote, wrote, scratching his foolscap noisily with a hurrying pen, straight through the paper. Dick envied him his fluency his readiness, his rapidity; the Born Poet kept his knowledge all packed for immediate use at the ends of his fingers, and seemed able to pour it forth, on no matter what topic, the very instant he required it. Words came to him quick as thought; he never paused for a second. Before the end of the examination Dick had long ago given up all for lost, and only went on writing at the papers at all from a dogged sense that it ill became a Plantagenet to admit he was beaten as long as a drop of blood or a whiff of breath remained in his body.

The three days of the examination passed slowly away, and each day Dick felt even more dissatisfied with his work than he had felt on the previous one. On the very last evening he indited a despondent letter to Maud, so as to break the disappointment for her gently, explaining how unequally he was matched with this clever fellow Gillingham, whom all Rugby regarded with unanimous voice as a heaven-sent genius, a natural historian, and a Born Poet. After which, with many sighs, he betook himself once more for the twentieth time to the study of the questions he had answered worst, wondering how on earth he could ever have made that stupid blunder about Aidan and the Synod of Whitby, and what could have induced him to suppose for one second that Peter of Amboise was really the same person as Peter the Hermit.. With these and other like errors he made his soul miserable that live-long night; and he worried himself with highly-coloured mental pictures of the disgrace he would feel it to return to Chiddingwick, no Oxford man at all, but a bookseller's assistant.

Not till twelve o'clock next day was the result to be announced. Richard spent the morning listlessly with Gillingham and Faussett. The Born Poet was not boastful; he hated ostentation; but he let it be clearly felt he knew he had acquitted himself with distinguished credit. Poor Dick was miserable. He half reflected upon the desirability of returning at once to Chiddingwick, without waiting to hear the result of the examination; but the blood of the Plantagenets revolted within him against such a confession of abject cowardice. At twelve o'clock or a little after he straggled round to Durham. In the big Chapel Quad a crowd of eager competitors gathered thick in front of the notice-board. Dick hardly dared to press in among them and read in plain black and white the story of his own unqualified discomfiture. He held back and hesitated. Two elderly men in caps and gowns, whom he knew now by sight as Fellows and Tutors, were talking to one another quite loud by the gate. 'But we haven't seen Plantagenet yet,' the gravest of them said to his neighbour; he was a tall fair man, with a cultivated red beard and a most aesthetic pince-nez. .

Dick's heart came up in his mouth. He stood forward diffidently.

'My name's Plantagenet,' he said, with a very white face. 'Did you want to speak to me?'

'Oh yes,' the Tutor answered, shaking him warmly by the hand; 'you must come up, you know, to enter your name on the books, and be introduced to the Warden.'

Dick trembled like a girl. His heart jumped within him.

'Why, what have I got?' he asked, hardly daring even to ask it, lest he should find himself mistaken.

The man with the red beard held out a duplicate copy of the paper on the notice-board.

'You can see for yourself,' he answered; and Dick looked at it much agitated.

'Modern History: Mr. Richard Plantagenet, late of Chiddingwick Grammar School, is elected to a Scholarship of the annual value of One Hundred Pounds. Proximo accessit, Mr. Trevor Gillingham, of Rugby School. Mr. Gillingham is offered a set of rooms, rent free, in the College.'

The world reeled round and round on Dick as a pivot. It was too good to be true. He couldn't even now believe it. Of what happened next he never had any clear or connected recollection. In some vague phantasmagoric fashion he was dimly aware of being taken by the Tutor into the College Hall and introduced by name to a bland-looking effigy in a crimson gown, supposed to represent the Head of the College; after which it seemed to him that somebody made him sign a large book of statutes or something of the sort in medieval Latin, wherein he described himself as 'Plantagenet, Ricardus, gen. fil., hujus ædis alumnus,' and that somebody else informed him in the same tongue he was duly elected. And then he bowed himself out in what Mr. Plantagenet the elder would have considered a painfully inadequate manner, and disappeared with brimming eyes into the front quadrangle.

As yet he had scarcely begun to be faintly conscious of a vague sense of elation and triumph; but as he reached the open air, which freshened and revived him, it occurred to him all at once that now he was really to all practical intents and purposes an Oxford undergraduate, one of those very people whose gorgeous striped blazers and lordly manners had of late so overawed him. Would he ever himself wear such noble neckties? Would he sport a straw hat with a particoloured ribbon? He looked up at the big window of that beautiful chapel, with its flamboyant tracery, and felt forthwith a proprietary interest in it. By the door Faussett was standing. As Dick passed he looked up and recognised 'the dark horse,' the rank outsider. He came forward and took his hand, which he wrung with unfeigned admiration.

'By Jove, Plantagenet,' he cried, 'you've licked us; you've fairly licked us! It's wonderful, old man. I didn't think you'd have done it. The Poet's such an extraordinary dab, you know, at history. But you must be a dabber. Look here, I say, what a pity you didn't take me the other day when I offered even money on Trev against the field! You simply chucked away a good chance of a fiver.'

A little further on, Gillingham himself strolled up to them. His manner was pure gold. There was no trace of jealousy in the way he seized his unexpected rival's hand. To do him justice, indeed, that smallest and meanest of the human passions had no place at all in the Born Poet's nature.

'Well, I congratulate you,' he said with a passing pang of regret, for he, too, had wished not a little to get that Scholarship; 'as Sir Philip Sidney said, your need was the greater. And even for myself I'm not wholly dissatisfied. It's been a disappointment to me, and I don't very often secure the luxury of a disappointment. The true poet, you see, ought to have felt and known every human passion, good, bad or indifferent. As pure; experience, therefore, I'm not sorry you've licked me. It will enable me to throw myself henceforth more dramatically and realistically into the position of the vanquished, which is always the more pathetic, and therefore the more poetical.'

They parted a little further down on the way towards the High Street. After they'd done so, the Philistine turned admiringly towards his schoolfellow, whom no loyal Rugby boy could for a moment believe to have been really beaten in fair fight by a creature from a place called Chiddingwick Grammar School.

'By George! Trev,' he exclaimed with a glow of genuine admiration, 'I never saw anything like that. It was noble, it was splendid of you!'

The Born Poet hardly knew what his companion meant; but if it meant that he thought something which he, Trevor Gillingham, had done was noble and splendid, why, 'twas certainly not the Born Poet's cue to dispute the point with him. So he smiled a quiet non-committing sort of smile, and murmured in a gentle but distant voice: 'Aha! you think so?'

'Think so!' Faussett echoed. 'Why, of course I do; it's magnificent. Only, for the honour of the school, you know, Trev, I really think you oughtn't to have done it. You ought to have tried your very best to lick him.'

'How did you find it out?' Trevor Gillingham asked languidly. He affected languor at times as an eminently poetic attitude.

'How did I find it out? Why, you as good as acknowledged it yourself when you said to him just now, "Your need was the greater." There aren't many, fellows who'd have done it, Trev, I swear; but it wasn't right, all the same; you've the school to consider; and you ought to have fought him through thick and thin for it!'

The Born Poet stroked his beardless chin with recovered self-satisfaction. This was a capital idea, a first-rate way out of it! For his own part, he had written all he knew, and tried his very best to get that Scholarship; but if Faussett chose to think he had deliberately given it away, out of pure quixotic goodness of heart, to his obscure competitor from Giggleswick School, or was the place called Chiddingwick?—whose need was the greater, why, it wasn't any business of his to correct or disclaim that slight misapprehension. And in three days more, indeed, it was the firm belief of every right-minded Rugby boy that 'Gillingham of our school' could easily have potted the Durham Scholarship if he'd chosen; but he voluntarily retired from the contest beforehand, morally scratched for it, so to speak, because he knew there was another fellow going in for the stakes 'whose need,' as he generously phrased it, 'was the greater.'

And meanwhile Dick Plantagenet himself, the real hero of the day, was straggling down, more dead than alive for joy, towards the Oxford postoffice, to send off the very first telegram he had ever despatched in his life:

'"Miss Maud Plantagenet, Chiddingwick, Surrey. Hooray! I've got it, the hundred pound history." Thirteen words: sixpence ha'penny. Strike out the Maud, and it's the even sixpence.'

CHAPTER VII - AFFAIRS OF THE HEART

The return to Chiddingwick was a triumphal entry. Before seven o'clock that evening, when the South-Eastern train crawled at its accustomed leisurely pace, with a few weary gasps, into Chiddingwick Station, Mr. Plantagenet had spread the news of his son's success broadcast through the town, viâ the White Horse parlour. Already, on the strength of Dick's great achievement, he had become the partaker, at other people's expense, of no fewer than three separate brandies-and-sodas; which simple Bacchic rites, more frequently repeated, would have left him almost incapable of meeting the hero of the hour with suitable effect, had not Maud impounded him, so to speak, by main force after five o'clock tea, and compelled him to remain under strict supervision in the domestic gaol till the eve of Dick's arrival.

Dick jumped out, all eagerness. On the platform his mother stood waiting to receive him, proud, but tearful; for to her, good woman, the glories of the Plantagenet name were far less a matter of interest than the thought of losing for the best part of three years the mainstay of the family. Maud was there, too, beaming over with pure delight, and even prouder than she had ever been in her life before of her handsome brother. Mr. Plantagenet himself really rose for once to the dignity, of the occasion, and instead of greeting Richard with the theatrical grace and professional flourish he had originally contemplated, forgot in the hurry of the moment the high-flown speech he had mentally composed for delivery on the platform, and only remembered to grasp his son's hand hard with genuine warmth as he murmured in some broken and inarticulate way: 'My boy, my dear boy, we're all so pleased and delighted to hear it.' He reflected afterwards, with regret, to be sure, that he had thrown away a magnificent opportunity for a most effective display by his stupid emotion; but Dick was the gainer by it. Never before in his life did he remember to have seen his father act or speak with so much simple and natural dignity.

All Chiddingwick, indeed, rejoiced with their joy. For Chiddingwick, we know, was proud in its way of the Plantagenets. Did not the most respectable families send their children to take dancing lessons at the White Horse Assembly Rooms from the disreputable old scamp, on the strength of his name, his faded literary character, and his shadowy claim to regal ancestry? The station-master himself, that mighty man in office, shook hands with 'Mr. Richard' immediately on his arrival; the porters presented him with a bouquet of white pinks fresh plucked from the Company's garden; and even Mr. Wells raised his hat to his late assistant with full consciousness of what respect was due from a country tradesman to a gentleman who had been admitted with flying colours to 'Oxford College.'

Dick's progress up the High Street was one long shaking of many friendly hands; and if that benevolent soul, Mr. Trevor Gillingham, of Rugby School, could only have seen the deep interest which his rival's success excited in an entire community, he would have felt more than ever, what he frequently told all his Sixth Form friends, that he was glad he'd been able 'practically to retire' in favour of a young man so popular and so deserving.

And then, after the first flush of delight in his victory had worn off, there grew up in Richard's mind the more practical question of ways and means. What was he to do with his time in the interval, till term began in October? Neither his father nor Mr. Wells would hear of his returning meanwhile to his old employment.

'No, no, Dick, Mr. Richard, I mean,' the good bookseller said seriously. 'For your sake and the business's, I couldn't dream of permitting it. It's out of place entirely. A scholar of Durham College, Oxford, mustn't soil his hands with waiting in a shop. It wouldn't be respectable. No self-respecting tradesman can have a gentleman in your present position standing behind his counter. I call it untradesmanlike. It's calculated to upset the natural and proper relations of classes. You must look out for some work more suited to your existing position and prospects; and I must look out for an assistant in turn who ain't a member of an ancient and respected University.'

Dick admitted with a sigh the eternal fitness of Mr. Wells's view; but, at the same time, he wondered what work on earth he could get which would allow him to earn his livelihood for the moment without interfering with the new and unpractical dignity of a Scholar of Durham College, Oxford. He had saved enough from his wages to eke out his Scholarship and enable him to live very economically at the University; but he must bridge over the time between now and October without trenching upon the little nest-egg laid by for the future.

As often happens, chance stepped in at the very nick of time to fill up the vacancy. At the Rectory that night Mr. Tradescant was talking over with his wife the question of a tutor for their eldest son, that prodigiously stupid boy of seventeen, a pure portent of ignorance, who was to go in for an army examination at the end of September.

'No, I won't send him away, from home, Clara,' the Rector broke out testily. 'It's no earthly use sending him away from home. He's far too lazy. Unless Arthur's under my own eye, he'll never work with anyone. Let me see, he comes home from Marlborough on the 28th. We must get somebody somehow before then who'll be able to give him lessons at home, if possible. If he has two months and more of perfect idleness he'll forget all he ever knew (which isn't much), and go up for examination with his mind a perfect blank, a tabula rasa, a sheet of white note-paper. And yet, unless we get a tutor down from town every day, which would run into money, I'm sure I don't know who the—person is we could possibly get to teach him.'

Mary Tudor was sitting by, and being a very young and inexperienced girl, she hadn't yet learnt that the perfect governess, when she hears her employers discuss their private affairs, should behave as though her ears wore only for ornament. (And Mary's, indeed, were extremely ornamental.) So she intervened with a suggestion, a thing no fully-trained young woman from a modern Agency would ever dream of doing.

'There's that Plantagenet boy, you know, Mrs. Tradescant,' she remarked, without bearing him the slightest grudge for his curious behaviour over the bookbinding incident. 'He's just got a Scholarship at Oxford to-day, Mr. Wells was telling me. I wonder if he would do? They say he's a very clever, well-read young fellow.'

The Reverend Hugh received the suggestion with considerable favour.

'Why, there's something in that, Miss Tudor,' he said, leaning back in his easy-chair. 'I'm glad you thought of it. The young man must be fairly well up in his work to have taken a Scholarship, a very good one, too, a hundred a year, at my own old college. I met Plantagenet this afternoon in the High Street overflowing with it. This is worth looking into, Clara. He's on the spot, you must bear in mind; and under the circumstances, I expect, he'd be in want of work, and willing, I daresay, to take extremely little. He can't very well go back to Wells's, don't you see, and he can't afford to live at home without doing something.'

'The boy's as mad as a March hare, and not a very desirable companion for Arthur, you must feel yourself,' Mrs. Tradescant answered a little chillily, not over well pleased with Mary for having ventured to interfere in so domestic a matter. 'And, besides, there's the old man. Just consider the associations!'

'Well, he can't help being the son of his father,' the Rector replied with a man's greater tolerance. 'He was born with that encumbrance. And as to companions, my dear, young Plantagenet's at any rate a vast deal better than Reece and the groom, who seem to me to be Arthur's chief friends and allies whenever he's at home here. The boy may be mad, as you suggest, I dare say he is, but he's not too mad to get a Durham Scholarship; and I only wish Arthur had half his complaint in that matter. A fellow who can take a scholarship at Durham's no fool, I can tell you. I'll inquire about his terms when I go into town to-morrow.' And the Reverend Hugh did inquire accordingly, and found Dick's attainments so satisfactory for his purpose that he forthwith engaged the new scholar as tutor for Arthur, to come five days in the week and give four hours' tuition a day till the end of September, at a most modest salary, which to Dick nevertheless seemed as the very wealth of Croesus. Not till long after did Dick know that he owed this appointment in the first instance to a chance word of

Mary Tudor's. Nor did Mary suspect, when, out of pure goodness of heart and sympathy for a deserving and struggling young man, she suggested him for the appointment, that his engagement would be the occasion of throwing them too much together in future.

So luck would have it, however. Five days a week Dick went up with his little strapped parcel of books to the Rectory door to engage in the uncongenial and well-nigh impossible task of endeavouring to drive the faint shadow of an idea into Arthur Tradescant's impenetrable cranium. It was work, hard work, but it had its compensations. For, quite insensibly to both at first, it brought Dick and Mary a great deal into one another's society at many odd moments. In the very beginning, it is true, they only met quite by accident in the hall and passages or on the garden path; and Mary rather shrank from conversation with the young man who had been the hero of that curious episode about the binding of the 'Flora.' But gradually the same chance threw them more and more into contact; besides, their relative positions had been somewhat altered meanwhile by Dick's success at Durham. He was now no longer the bookseller's young man, but a student who was shortly to go up to Oxford. This told with Mary, as it tells with all of us, almost without our knowing it. We can seldom separate the man from the artificial place he holds in our social system. Indeed, the very similarity of their positions in the household, his as tutor and hers as governess, made to some extent now a bond of union between them. Before many weeks were out Mary had begun to look for Dick's pleasant smile of welcome when he arrived in the morning, and to see that the strange young man, whose grave demeanour and conscious self-respect had struck her so markedly that first day at Mr. Wells's, had really after all a great deal in him.

The more Dick saw of Mary, too, the better he liked her. Just at first, to be sure, his impulse had been a mere freak of fancy, based on the curious coincidence of their regal names; that alone, and nothing else, had made him think to himself he might possibly fall in love with her. But after awhile the mere fancy counted for comparatively little; it was the woman herself, bright, cheery, sensible, that really attracted him. From the very beginning he had admired her; he soon learned to love her; and Mary, for her part, found it pleasant, indeed, that there was somebody in this social wilderness of Chiddingwick who genuinely cared for her. A governess's lot is as a rule a most lonely one, and sympathy in particular is passing dear to her. Now Dick was able to let Mary feel he sympathized with her silently in her utter loneliness; and Mary grew soon to be grateful to Dick in turn for his kindness and attention. She forgot the handsome shopman with the long, yellow hair in the prospective glories of the Durham undergraduate.

The summer wore away, and the time drew near when Richard must begin to think about his preparations for going up to Oxford. A day or two before the date fixed for the meeting of the colleges, he was walking on the footpath that runs obliquely across the fields which stretch up the long slope of the hill behind Chiddingwick.

As he walked and reflected, he hardly noticed a light figure in a pretty print dress hurrying down the hillside towards him. As it approached, he looked up; a sudden thrill ran through him. It was Mary who was coming! How odd! He had been thinking about her that very moment! And yet not so odd, either; for how often he thought about her! He had been thinking just now that he couldn't bear to leave Chiddingwick without telling her how much she had lately become to him, and how very, very deeply he regretted leaving her. His face flushed at the sight and the thought; it seemed to him almost like an omen of success that she should happen to come up at the very moment when he was thinking such things of her. It was so unusual for Mary to go out beyond the Rectory grounds by herself; still more unusual for her to be coming home alone so late in that particular direction. He raised his hat as she approached. 'Oh, Miss Tudor,' he cried shyly, with a young man's mixture of timidity and warmth, 'I'm so glad to see you here. I—I was just thinking about you. I want to have a talk with you.'

'And I was just thinking about you,' Mary answered more frankly, with a scarcely perceptible blush—the charming blush that comes over a good girl's face when she ventures to say something really kind and sympathetic to a man she cares for. 'I was thinking how very soon we're going to lose you.' And as she said it, she reflected to herself what a very different young man this pleasant intelligent Oxford scholar seemed to her now from the singular person who had insisted, three months back, on putting her monogram with the Tudor rose on the 'British Flora'!

'No, were you really?' Dick cried, with a glowing cheek, much deeper red than her own. 'Now that was just kind of you. You can't think how much pleasanter and happier in every way you've made my time at the Rectory for me.' And he glanced down into her liquid eyes with grateful devotion.

'I might say the same thing to you,' Mary answered, very low, hardly knowing whether it was quite right of her even to admit such reciprocity.

Dick's face was on fire with ingenuous delight.

'No, you can't mean to say that?' he exclaimed, a delicious little thrill coursing through him to the finger-tips. 'Oh, how very, very kind of you!' He hesitated a moment; then he added with a tremor: 'You needn't walk so fast, you know. I may just turn round and walk back with you, mayn't I?'

'I don't quite know,' Mary answered, looking round her, a little uncertain. She didn't feel sure in her own heart whether she ought to allow him. He was a very nice fellow, to be sure, and she liked him immensely, now she'd got to know him; but would Mrs. Tradescant approve of her permitting him to accompany her? 'Perhaps you'd better not,' she faltered again; but her lingering tones belied her words. 'I'm—I'm in a hurry to get home. I really mustn't wait a minute.'

In spite of what she said, however, Dick continued, just like a man, to walk on by her side; and Mary, it must be admitted by the candid historian, took no great pains to prevent him. 'I'm so glad you say you'll miss me, Miss Tudor,' he began timidly, after a very long pause, oh, those eloquent pauses! 'For. I too shall miss you.

We've seen so much of each other, you know, these last six or eight weeks; and it's been such a pleasure to me.'

Mary answered nothing, but walked on faster than ever, as if in particular haste to return to the Rectory, where they were really awaiting her. Still, a great round spot burned bright red in her cheek, and her poor throbbing heart gave a terrible flutter.

Dick tried to slacken the pace, but Mary wouldn't allow him. 'Do you know,' he went on, glancing down at her appealingly, 'it may seem a queer thing to you for a fellow to say, but until I met you, my sister Maud was the only girl I'd ever met whom I could consider, well, my equal.'

He said it quite simply, with all the pride of a Plantagenet; and as he spoke, Mary felt conscious to herself that, whatever else Dick might be, after all he was a gentleman. Yes, and, in spite of old Mr. Plantagenet's many obvious faults, a descendant of gentlemen too; for even in his last disreputable and broken old age traces of breeding still clung about the Chiddingwick dancing-master. Mary instinctively understood and sympathized with the poor lad's feeling. She spoke very softly. 'I know what you mean,' she said, 'and I can understand it with you. I've met your sister—at—the White Horse, and I felt, of course—'

She checked herself suddenly. She had just been going to say, 'I felt she was a lady,' but instinct taught her at once how rude and pretentious the expression would sound to him; so she altered her unspoken phrase to, 'I felt at once we should have a great deal in common.'

'I'm so glad you think so,' Dick murmured in return, growing fiery red once more, for he knew Mary was accustomed to accompany the Rectory children to the Assembly Rooms dancing lessons, where Maud' often helped her father with her violin; and he couldn't bear to think she should have seen the head of the house engaged in such an unworthy and degrading occupation. 'Well, I was just going to say, you're the only girl I ever met in my life with whom I could speak, you know what I mean, why, just speak my whole heart out.'

'It's very kind of you to say so,' Mary answered, beginning to walk much faster. She was really getting frightened now what Dick might go on to say to her.

'And so,' the young man continued, floundering on after the fashion of young men in love, 'I—I shall feel going away from you.'

Mary's heart beat fast. She liked Dick very much, oh, very much indeed; but she didn't feel quite sure it was anything more than liking. (Women, you know, make in these matters such nice distinctions.) 'You'll meet plenty of new friends,' she said faintly, 'at Oxford.'

'Oh, but that won't be at all the same!' Dick answered, trembling. 'They'll all be men, you see.' And then he paused, wondering whether perhaps he had spoken too plainly.

Mary's pace by this time had become almost unladylike, so fast was she walking. Still, just to break the awkward silence which followed Dick's last words, she felt compelled to say something. 'You'll meet plenty of girls, too, I expect,' she interposed nervously.

'Perhaps; but they won't be you,' Dick blurted out with a timid gasp, gazing straight into her eyes; and then recoiled, aghast, at his own exceeding temerity.

Mary blushed again and cast down her eyes. 'Don't let me take you out of your way any farther,' she said after another short pause, just to cover her confusion. 'I really must get back now. Mrs. Tradescant'll be so angry.'

'Oh no; you can't go just yet!' Dick cried, growing desperate, and standing half across the path, with a man's masterful eagerness. 'Now I've once begun with it, I must say my say out to you. Miss Tudor, that very first day I ever saw you, I thought a great deal of you. You could tell I did by the mere fact that I took the trouble to make such a fool of myself over that unhappy book-cover. But the more I've seen of you, the better I've liked you. Liked you, oh, so much I can hardly tell you! And when I went up to Oxford about this Scholarship, which has given me a start in life, I thought about you so often that I really believe I owe my success in great part to you. Now, what I want to say before I go'—he paused and hesitated; it was so hard to word it—'what I want to say's just this. Perhaps you'll think it presumptuous of me; but do you feel, if I get on, and recover the place in the world that belongs by right to my family, do you feel as if there's any chance you might ever be able to care for me?'

He jerked it out, all trembling. Mary trembled herself, and hardly knew what to answer; for though she liked the young man very much, more than any other young man she'd ever yet met, she hadn't thought of him to herself in this light exactly, at least, not very often. So she stood for a moment in the corner of the path by that bend in the field where the hedge hides and shelters one, and replied diplomatically, with sound feminine common-sense, though with a quiver in her voice:

'Don't you think, Mr. Plantagenet, it's a little bit premature for you to talk of these things when you're only just going up to Oxford? For your own sake, you know, and your family's too, you ought to leave yourself as free and untrammelled as possible: you oughtn't to burden yourself beforehand with uncertainties and complications.'

Dick looked at her half reproachfully. 'Oh, Miss Tudor!' he cried, drawing back quite seriously, 'I wouldn't allow anybody else in the world to call you a complication.'

He said it so gravely that Mary laughed outright in spite of herself. But Dick was very much in earnest, for all that. 'I mean it, though,' he went on, hardly smiling to himself. 'I mean it, most literally. I want you to tell me, before I go up to Oxford, there's still some chance, some little chance in the future for me. Or at any rate I want to let you know what I feel, so that—well, so that if anybody else should speak to you meanwhile, you will remember at least—and—'

He broke off suddenly. 'Oh, Miss Tudor,' he cried once more, looking down at her with a mutely appealing look, 'it means so much to me!'

'You're very young, you know,' Mary answered, with a good woman's subterfuge, half to gain time. 'I think it would be very foolish, both for you and me, to tie ourselves down at our present ages. And besides, Mr. Plantagenet'—she played with her parasol a moment—'I don't want to hurt your feelings, but I'm not quite sure—whether or not I care for you.'

There was a tremor in her voice that made her words mean less than they seemed to mean; but she felt it too. This was all so sudden. Nevertheless, Dick seized her hand. She tried to withdraw it, but couldn't. Then he began in eager tones to pour forth his full heart to her. He knew he had no right to ask, but he couldn't bear to go away and leave the chance of winning her open to some other fellow. It must be for a very long time, of course; but, still, he could work better if he knew he was working for her. He didn't want her to say 'Yes'; he only wanted her not quite to say 'No' outright to him. This, and much else, he uttered from his heart with rapidly developing eloquence. He was so glad he'd met her, for he couldn't have left Chiddingwick without at least having spoken to her.

To all which Mary, with downcast eyes, very doubtful, though she liked him, whether it was quite right for her to talk in this strain at all to the dancing-master's son, replied demurely that 'twas all very premature, and that she didn't feel able to give him any answer of any sort, either positive or negative, till they had both of them had more time to look about them.

'And now,' she said finally, pulling out her watch, and starting, 'I really mustn't stop one moment longer. I must go back at once. It's dreadfully late. I'm sure I don't know what Mrs. Tradescant will think of me.'

'At least,' Dick cried, standing half in front of her yet again, and blocking up the pathway, 'you'll allow me to write to you?'

Yes, Mary thought, yielding, there'd be no harm in that, no objection to his writing.

Dick gave a little sigh of heartfelt satisfaction. 'Well, that's something!' he cried, much relieved. 'That's always something! If you'll allow me to write to you, I shall feel at any rate you can't quite forget me.'

And, indeed, when a girl lets a young man begin a correspondence, experience teaches me, from long observation, that other events are not unlikely to follow.

CHAPTER VIII - AT 'OXFORD COLLEGE'

Well, I don't know what you fellows think, but as far as I'm concerned,' Trevor Gillingham remarked, with an expansive wave of his delicate white hand, 'my verdict on the Last of the Plantagenets is simply this: the Prince of the Blood has been weighed in the balance and found wanting.'

It was a fortnight later, in Faussett's rooms in the Chapel Quad at Durham (Chapel Quad is the most fashionably expensive quarter), and a party of raw lads, who took themselves for men, all gathered round their dessert, were engaged in discussing their fellow-undergraduate. The table groaned with dried fruits and mandarin oranges. Faussett himself raised to his lips a glass of Oxford wine-merchant's sherry, 'our famous Amontillado as imported, thirty-six shillings the dozen', and observed in a tone of the severest criticism: 'Oh, the man's a smug; a most unmitigated smug: that's the long and the short of it.'

Now, to be a smug is, in Oxford undergraduate circles, the unpardonable sin. It means, to stop in your own rooms and moil and toil, or to lurk and do nothing, while other men in shoals are out and enjoying themselves. It means to avoid the river and the boats; to shun the bump-supper; to decline the wine-party. Sometimes, it is true, the smug is a curmudgeon; but sometimes he is merely a poor and hard-working fellow, the sort of person whom at forty we call a man of ability.

'Well, I won't go quite so far as that,' one of the other lads observed, smacking his lips with an ostentatious air of judicial candour, about equally divided between Dick and the claret. 'I won't quite condemn him as a smug, unheard. But it's certainly odd he shouldn't join the wine-club.'

He was a second-year man, the speaker, one Westall by name, who had rowed in the Torpids; and as the rest were mostly freshmen of that term, his opinion naturally carried weight with all except Gillingham. He, indeed, as a Born Poet, was of course allowed a little more license in such matters than his even Christians.

'Up till now,' Faussett put in, with a candid air of historical inquiry, 'you see every Durham man has always as a matter of course subscribed to the wine-club. Senior men tell me they never knew an exception.'

Gillingham looked up from his easy-chair with a superior smile. 'I don't object to his not joining it,' he said, with a curl of the cultured lip, for the Born Poet of course represented culture in this scratch collection of ardent young Philistines; 'but why, in the name of goodness, didn't he say outright like a man he couldn't afford it? It's the base hypocrisy of his putting his refusal upon moral grounds, and calling himself a total abstainer, that sets my back up. If a man's poor in this world's goods, and can't afford to drink a decent wine, in heaven's name let him say so; but don't let him go snuffling about, pretending he doesn't care for it, or he doesn't want it, or he doesn't like it, or he wouldn't take it if he could get it. I call that foolish and degrading, as well as unmanly. Even Shakespeare himself used to frequent the Mermaid tavern. Why, where would all our poetry be, I should like to know, if it weren't for Bacchus? Bacchus, ever fair and ever young? "War, he sang, is toil and trouble; Honour but an empty bubble; Never ending, still beginning; Fighting still, and still destroying; If the world be worth thy winning, Think, oh, think it worth enjoying."'

And Gillingham closed his eyes ecstatically as he spoke, and took another sip at the thirty-six Amontillado, in a rapture of divine poesy.

'Hear, hear!' Faussett cried, clapping his hands with delight. 'The Born Poet for a song! The Born Poet for a recitation! You men should just hear him spout "Alexander's Feast." It's a thing to remember! He's famous as a spouter, don't you know, at Rugby. Why, he's got half the British poets or more by heart, and a quarter of the prose authors. He can speak whole pages. But "Alexander's Feast" is the thing he does the very best of all. Whenever he recites it he brings the house down.'

'Respect for an ancient and picturesque seat of learning prevents me from bringing down the roof of Durham College, then,' Gillingham answered lightly, with a slight sneer for his friend's boyish enthusiasm. 'Besides, my dear boy, you wander from the subject. When the French farmer asked his barn-door fowls to decide with what sauce they would wish to be eaten, they held a meeting of their own in the barton-yard, and sent their spokesman to say, "If you please, M. le Propriétaire, we very much prefer not to be eaten."

"Mes amis," said the farmer, "vous vous écartez de la question." And that's your case, Faussett. The business before the house is the moral turpitude and mental obliquity of the man Plantagenet, who refuses, as he says, on conscientious grounds, to join the college wine-club. Now, I take that as an insult to a society of gentlemen.'

'What a lark it would be,' Faussett cried, 'if we were to get him up here just now, offer him some wine, to which he pretends he has a conscientious objection, unless somebody else pays for it, make him drink success to the cause of total abstinence, keep filling up his glass till we make him dead drunk, and then set him at the window in a paper cap to sing "John Barleycorn."'

Gillingham's thin lip curled visibly. 'Your humour, my dear boy,' he said, patting Faussett on the back, 'is English, English, essentially English. It reminds me of Gilray. It lacks point and fineness. Your fun is like your neckties, loud, too loud! You must cultivate your mind (if any) by a diligent study of the best French models. I would recommend, for my part, as an efficient antidote, a chapter of De Maupassant and an ode of François Coppée's every night and morning.'

'But if Plantagenet's poor,' one more tolerant lad put in apologetically, 'it's natural enough, after all, he shouldn't want to join the club. It's precious expensive, you know, Gillingham. It runs into money.'

The Born Poet was all sweet reasonableness.

'To be poor, my dear Matthews,' he said, with a charming smile, turning round to the objector, 'as Beau Brummell remarked about a rent in one's coat, is an accident that may happen to any gentleman any day; but a patch, you must recognise, is premeditated poverty. The man Plantagenet may be as poor as he chooses, so far as I'm concerned; I approve of his being poor. What so picturesque, so affecting, so poetical, indeed, as honest poverty? But to pretend he doesn't care for wine, that's quite another matter. There the atrocity comes in, the vulgarian atrocity. For I call such a statement nothing short of vulgar.' He raised his glass once more, and eyed the light of the lamp through the amethystine claret with poetic appreciation. 'Now give the hautboys breath,' he cried, breaking out once more in a fit of fine dithyrambic inspiration; 'he comes! he comes! Bacchus, ever fair and ever young, Drinking joys did first ordain. Bacchus' blessings are a treasure; Drinking is the soldier's pleasure. Rich the tr-r-reasure. Sweet the pleasure. Sweet is pleasure after pain.'

And when Gillingham said that, with his studiously unstudied air of profound afflatus, everybody in the company felt convinced at once that Plantagenet's teetotalism, real or hypocritical, simply hadn't got a leg left to stand upon. They turned for consolation to the Carlsbad plums and the candied cherries.

But at the very same moment, in those more modest rooms, up two pair of stairs in the Back Quad, which Dick had selected for himself as being the cheapest then vacant, the Prince of the Blood himself sat in an old stuffed chair, in a striped college boating coat, engaged in discussing his critic Gillingham in a more friendly spirit with a second-year man, who, though not a smug, was a reader and a worker, by name Gillespie, a solid Glasgow Scotchman. They had rowed together that afternoon in a canvas pair to Sandford, and now they were working in unison on a chapter or two of Aristotle.

'For my own part,' Dick said, 'when I hear Gillingham talk, I'm so overwhelmed with his knowledge of life and his knowledge of history, and his extraordinary reading, that I feel quite ashamed to have carried off the Scholarship against him. I feel the examiners must surely have made a mistake, and some day they'll find it out, and be sorry they elected me.'

'You needn't be afraid of that,' Gillespie answered, smiling, and filling his pipe. 'You lack the fine quality of a "guid conceit o' yoursel," Plantagenet. I've talked a bit with Gillingham now and again, and I don't think very much of him. He's not troubled that way. He's got an extraordinary memory, and a still more extraordinary opinion of his own high merits; but I don't see, bar those two, that there's anything particularly brilliant or original about him. He's a poet, of course, and he writes good verses. Every fellow can write good verses nowadays. The trick's been published. All can raise the flower now, as Tennyson puts it, for all have got the seed. But, as far as I can judge Gillingham, his memory's just about the best thing about him. He has a fine confused lot of undigested historical knowledge packed away in his head loose; but he hasn't any judgment; and judgment is ability. The examiners were quite right, my dear fellow; you know less than Gillingham in a way; but you know it more surely, and you can make better use of it. His work's showy and flashy; yours is solid and serviceable.'

And Gillespie spoke the truth. Gradually, as Dick got to see more of the Born Poet's method, he found Gillingham out; he discovered that the great genius was essentially a poseur. He posed about everything. His rôle in life, he said himself, was to be the typical poet; and he never forgot it. He dressed the part; he acted it; he ate and drank poetically. He looked at everything from the point of view of a budding Shakespeare, with just a dash of Shelley thrown in, and a suspicion of Matthew Arnold to give modern flavour. Add a tinge of Baudelaire, Victor Hugo, Ibsen, for cosmopolitan interest, and you have your bard complete. He was a spectator of the drama of human action, he loved to remark; he watched the poor creatures and the pretty creatures at their changeful game, doing, loving, and suffering. He saw in it all good material for his art, the raw stuff for future plays to astonish humanity. Meanwhile, he lay low at Durham College, Oxford, and let the undergraduate world deploy itself before him in simple Bacchic guise or Heraclean feats of strength and skill.

Dick saw more of Gillespie those first few terms than of anyone else in college. He was a thorough good fellow, Archibald Gillespie, and he had just enough of that ballast of common-sense and knowledge of the world which was a trifle lacking to the romantic country-bred lad fresh up from Chiddingwick. He helped Dick much with his work, and went much with him on the river. And Dick worked with a will at his history all that year, and pulled an oar with the best of them; though he found time, too, to coach a fellow-undergraduate going in for 'Smalls,' which increased his income by ten whole pounds, an incredible sum to him. When he thought of how hard it used to be to earn ten pounds at Mr. Wells's in the High Street at Chiddingwick, no wonder Oxford seemed to him a veritable Eldorado.

In spite of hard work, however, and frequent tight places, that first term at Oxford was a genuine delight to him. Who that has known it does not look back upon his freshman year, even in middle life, with regretful enjoyment? Those long mornings in great lecture-rooms, lighted up with dim light from stained-glass windows; those golden afternoons on the gleaming river or among the fields towards Iffey; those strolls round the leafy avenues of Christ Church walks; those loitering moments in Magdalen cloisters! What lounging in a punt under the chestnuts by the Cherwell; what spurts against the stream on the river by Godstow! All, all is delightful to the merest full-blooded boy; to Richard Plantagenet's romantic mind, stored with images of the past, 'twas a perpetual feast of fantastic pleasure.

He wrote to Mary twice a week. He would have written every day, indeed, if Mary had allowed him; but the lady of his love more prudently remarked that Mrs. Tradescant would be tempted to inquire in that case as to the name and business of her constant correspondent: He wrote her frankly all his joys and griefs, and she in return quite as frankly sympathized with him. Boy and girl as they were, it was all very pleasant. To be sure, it was understood and arranged on both sides beforehand by the high contracting parties that these letters were to be taken as written on purely friendly grounds, and, as the lawyers say, 'without prejudice'; still, as time went on, they grew more and more friendly, until at last it would have required the critical eye of an expert in breach-of-promise cases to distinguish them at first sight from ordinary love-letters. Indeed, just once, towards the end of term, Dick went so far as to begin one short note, 'Dearest Mary,' which was precisely what he always called her to himself in his own pleasant day-dreams; and then he had the temerity to justify his action in so many words by pleading the precedent of this purely mental usage. But Mary promptly put a stop to such advances by severely beginning her reply, 'Dear Mr. Plantagenet'; though, to be sure, she somewhat spoilt the moral effect of so stern a commencement by confessing at once in the sequel that she had headed her first draught with a frank 'Dear Dick,' and then torn it up, after all, being ashamed to send it.

When Dick read that deliciously feminine confession, consigned in blushing ink to fair white maiden notepaper, his heart gave a jump that might have been heard in Tom Quad, and his face grew as red as Mary's own when she penned it.

CHAPTER IX - A SUDDEN RESOLVE

Now, then, young gentlemen, choose your partners!' Mr. Plantagenet murmured with a bland and inane smile. ('Strike up the violin, Maud!' aside.) 'Bow, and fall into places. Eight bars before beginning. No, not yet, Miss Tradescant. Explain to this young lady, if you please, Miss Tudor, that she must always wait eight bars, eight bars exactly, before she begins to chasser. That's right. Just so! Advance in couples—right, left—right, left—right, left—down the middle. Very nicely done, indeed: very nicely, very nicely. Now!—yes—that's it. Change hands, and over again!'

A year and more had passed, and Mr. Plantagenet's face bore distincter signs than ever of his ruling passion. It was coarse and red under the bland exterior. Maud watched him intently now on the morning of lesson days to see he didn't slink away unobserved into the bar of the White Horse before the appointed hour for the meeting in the Assembly Rooms. Once let him cross the threshold of the inn, except to enter the big hall where he received his pupils, and all was up with him. On such occasions Maud was compelled with grief and shame to stick a notice on the door: 'Mr. Plantagenet is indisposed to-day, and will be unable to meet his usual classes.' Nobody else ever knew what agony those notices cost the poor shrinking girl; but on the next appointed afternoon Mr. Plantagenet would be at his place again as if nothing had happened, and would murmur plaintively, with one hand on his left breast and the other on the bow of his faithful violin:

'My old complaint, ladies and gentlemen, my old complaint! I suffer so much from my heart. I regret I was unable to receive you on Wednesday.' Everybody in Chiddingwick knew quite well the real nature of Mr. Plantagenet's 'old complaint,' but he was an institution of the place, and everybody pretended to believe in it and to sympathize with him.

On this particular day, however, in the middle of November, Mr. Plantagenet seemed even more consequential and more dignified than usual, if such a thing were possible. He received Lady Agatha's little girls with princely condescension. Maud, who stood by trembling, and watching him with dismay, as he fiddled with a will on his well-tried violin, wondered to herself, with a mute feeling of terror in her heart, what on earth could have put her father into such visible good humour. She didn't discover the secret till the end of the lesson. Then Mr. Plantagenet, rising with great importance and a conscious smirk, observed in his suavest and most professional tone:

'I am sorry to say, young ladies and gentlemen, and you, Miss Tudor, I won't be able to give the usual lessons next Tuesday and Wednesday. The fact of the matter is, I shall be away from Chiddingwick. It doesn't often happen that I take a holiday; but on this occasion I shall be away from Chiddingwick. Long and close attention to the duties of a harassing and wearisome task has undermined my constitution; you can sympathize with my feelings, and next week I propose to give myself a well-earned repose in order to visit my dear son at the University of Oxford.'

It was a perfect bombshell. To Maud, sitting by wearily, with her small violin clasped in her bloodless hands, the announcement came like a thunderbolt. He was going to Oxford! She turned deadly pale at once, and clutched the bow of her instrument with a spasmodic action. Mary Tudor, sitting near, noticed the pallor on her cheek, and guessed the cause of it instantly. The two girls looked up; for a second their eyes met, then Maud let hers drop suddenly. Though on that one dearest point Dick had never taken her into his confidence, Maud had guessed the whole truth during last Christmas vacation, and if anything could make the cup of her bitterness even bitterer than it was, 'twas the thought that Dick's friend, Dick's future wife, perhaps, should see and understand the full depths of her misery.

Mary had tact enough and feeling enough, however, not to press her sympathy upon the poor wounded creature. With a hasty side-glance she hurried her charges out of the room as quick as she could, and motioned to the other governesses to do the same for theirs with all possible expedition. Two minutes later the big hall was fairly cleared, and father and daughter stood face to face in silence.

If Maud had followed only the prompting of her own personal feelings, she would have sat down where she was, covered her face with her hands, and cried long and bitterly.

But her sense of duty towards her father prevented her from so giving way. She couldn't bear to let him see how deeply, for Dick's sake, she dreaded the idea of his going to Oxford. All she could do was to look up at him with a scared white face, and murmur in a terrified, half-articulate tone: 'Oh, father, father, you never told me of this! What on earth do you mean by it?'

Mr. Plantagenet eyed his daughter askance out of the corner of his eyes. He was more afraid of Maud than of anyone else on earth; in point of fact, she was his domestic keeper. But he tried to assume his jaunty, happy-go-lucky air, for all that.

'Well, my dear,' he said, examining the strings of his fiddle with profound attention, 'I haven't had a holiday for a very long time, away from Chiddingwick, and I'm tired with the duties, the duties of my very exacting profession, and I felt I needed a change, and I haven't been up to Oxford since your brother Richard entered into residence as a member of the University. Now, I naturally feel a desire to see my son in that position in life which a Plantagenet ought to occupy. And so, the long and the short of it is,' Mr. Plantagenet went on, shuffling about, and glancing up at her anxiously, 'the long and the short of it is, as you heard me inform my class just now, I think next week of allowing myself the luxury of a trip to Oxford.'

Maud rose and seized his arm. His grandeur and indefiniteness positively alarmed her. Did he think she would be taken in by such grandiose words?

'Now, father,' she said boldly, 'that sort of talk won't do between us two, you know, at a serious crisis. This is important, very. You must tell me quite plainly what you mean by it all. Does Dick know you're coming, and why do you want to go to him?'

Mr. Plantagenet, thus attacked, produced from his pocket a rather dirty silk handkerchief, and began to whimper. 'Has it come to this, then?' he cried with theatrical pathos; 'has it come to this, I ask you, that I, the head of all the Plantagenets, have to beg leave and make explanations to my own eldest daughter before I can go to visit my own son at Oxford?' and he hid his face in the pocket-handkerchief with a studied burst of emotion.

But Maud was inexorable. Dick's happiness was at stake. Not for worlds, if she could help it, would she have him shamed by the appearance before all the world of Oxford of that shabby, degraded, disreputable old man in the guise of his father.

'We must be practical,' she said coldly, taking no notice of his hysterics. 'You must explain what this means. I want to know all about it. How have you got money to go up to Oxford with, and all those bills unpaid, and Mrs. Waite still dunning us for the rent from last quarter? And where are you going to stop? And does Richard know you're coming? And have you proper things to go in? Why, I should think the very pride of a Plantagenet ought to prevent you from going to a place where your son lives like a gentleman, as he is, unless you can afford to go in such clothes as won't disgrace him!'

Thus put upon his mettle, Mr. Plantagenet, deeply moved, at first admitted by slow degrees that he had taken proper steps to replenish his wardrobe for this important occasion. He had ordered a suit of good clothes, very good clothes, at Wilkins's. And they would be paid for, too, the Head of the House added proudly. Oh, he wasn't quite so devoid of friends and resources in his old age as his undutiful daughter appeared to imagine. He could sometimes do a thing or two on his own account without asking her assistance. He had money in hand, loads, plenty of money for the journey!

'The more high-flown and enigmatical Mr. Plantagenet grew, the more terribly was poor Maud distressed and frightened. At last she could stand it no longer. Plantagenet though she was, and as proud as Heaven makes them, she couldn't prevent the tears from stealing through and betraying her. She flung herself into a chair and took her face in her hands.

'Now, father,' she said simply, giving way at last, 'you must tell me what you mean by it. You must explain the whole thing. Where did you get this money?'

Then, bit by bit, hard pressed, Mr. Plantagenet admitted, with many magnificent disclaimers and curious salves to his offended dignity, how he had become seized of a sum of unexpected magnitude. When he took the last rent of the Assembly Rooms, for the afternoon dancing-lessons, to the landlord of the White Horse, a fortnight earlier, the landlord had given him a receipt in full, and then, to his great surprise, had handed him back the money.

'You've been an old customer to me, Mr. Plantagenet,' Barnes had said, 'with real feeling, my dear, I assure you, with very real feeling'—'and a good customer, too, and a customer one could reckon upon, both for the Rooms and the parlour; and I feel, sir, now your son's gone up to Oxford College, and you a gentleman born, and so brought up, in the manner of speaking, it 'ud be a comfort to you, and a comfort to him, if you was to go up and see him. This 'ere little matter of the quarter's rent ain't nothing to me: you've brought me in as much and more in your time, as I says to my missus, with your conversational faculties. It draws people to the house, that it do, when they know there's a gent there of your conversational faculties.'

So, in the end, Mr. Plantagenet, after some decent parley, had accepted the gift, 'in the spirit in which it was offered, my dear, in the spirit in which it was offered,' and had resolved to apply it to the purpose which the donor indicated, as a means of paying a visit to Bichard at Oxford.

Poor Maud! she sat there heart-broken. She didn't know what to do. Pure filial feeling made her shrink from acknowledging, even to her own wounded soul, how ashamed she was of her father; far more did it prevent her from letting the poor broken old drunkard himself too plainly perceive it. All she could do was to sit there in blank despair, her hands folded before her, and reflect how all the care and pains she had taken to keep the rent-money sacred from his itching hands had only resulted at last in this supreme discomfiture. It was terrible, terrible! And Dick, she knew, had had social difficulties to contend with at Oxford at first, and was now just overcoming them, and beginning to be recognised as odd, very odd, but a decent sort of fellow. Mr. Plantagenet's visit would put an end to all that. He couldn't be kept sober for three days at a stretch; and he would disgrace dear Dick before the whole University.

However, Maud saw at once remonstrance was impossible. All she could conceivably do was to warn Dick beforehand. Forewarned is forearmed. She must warn Dick beforehand. Sorrowfully she went off by herself towards the post-office in the High Street. She would send a telegram. And then, even as she thought it, the idea came over her, how could she ever allow that fuzzy-headed Miss Janson at the Chiddingwick office to suspect the depth of the family disgrace? and another plan suggested itself. The third-class fare to Broughton, the next town of any size, was eightpence-ha'penny return: telegram would be sixpence; one and twopence-ha'penny in all: that was a lot of money! But still, for Dick's sake, she must venture upon the extravagance. With a beating heart in her breast, she hurried down to the station and took a ticket for Broughton. All the way there she was occupied in making up a telegram that should not compromise Richard; for she imagined to herself that a scholar of Durham would be a public personage of such distinction at Oxford that the telegraph clerks would be sure to note and retail whatever was said to him. At last, after infinite trials, she succeeded in satisfying herself.

'Plantagenet: Durham College, Oxford. E. P. visits Oxford to-morrow as surprise. Take precautions.—Maud.'

That came to sevenpence. But try as she would, she couldn't make it any shorter. Not for worlds would she describe E. P.'s relationship to the Scholar of Durham. And she blushed to herself as she handed it in to think she should have to ask the brother of whom she was so proud to take precautions against a visit from their own father!

CHAPTER X - MR. PLANTAGENET LIVES AGAIN

Outside college that same afternoon Trevor Gillingham, in a loud check suit, lounged lazily by the big front gate—on the prowl, as he phrased it himself, for an agreeable companion. For the Born Poet was by nature a gregarious animal, and hated to do anything alone, if a comrade could be found for him. But being a person of expansive mind, ever ready to pick up hints from all and sundry, he preferred to hook himself on by pure chance to the first stray comer, a process which contributed an agreeable dramatic variety to the course of his acquaintanceships. He loved deliberately to survey the kaleidoscope of life, and to try it anew in ever-varying combinations.

Now, the first man who emerged from the big gate that afternoon happened, as luck would have it, to be Richard Plantagenet, in his striped college blazer, on his way to the barges. Gillingham took his arm at once, as if they were boon companions.

'Are you engaged this afternoon?' he inquired with quite friendly interest. 'Because, if not, I should so much like the advantage of your advice and assistance. My governor's coming up next week for a few days to Oxford, and he wants some rooms, nice rooms to entertain in. He won't go to the Randolph, banal, very, don't you know, because he'll want to see friends a good deal. He's convivial, the governor; and he'd like a place where they'd be able to cook a decent dinner. Now, Edward Street would do, I should think. First-rate rooms in Edward Street. Can you come round and help me?'

He said it with an amount of empressement that was really flattering. Now, Dick had nothing particular to do that afternoon, though he had been bound for the river; but he always liked a stroll with that brilliant Gillingham, whom he had never ceased to admire as a creature from another social sphere, a cross between Lord Byron and the Admirable Crichton. So he put off his row, and walked round to Edward Street, the most fashionable quarter for high-class lodgings to be found in Oxford. Sir Bernard, it seemed, had just returned to England for a few short weeks from his Roumanian mission, and was anxious to get decent rooms, his son said, 'the sort of rooms, don't you know, where one can dine one's women folk, for he knows all the dons' families.' They looked at half a dozen sets, all in the best houses, and Gillingham finally selected a suite at ten guineas. Dick opened his eyes with astonishment at that lordly figure: he never really knew till then one could pay so much for lodgings. But he concealed his surprise from the Born Poet, his own pride having early taught him that great lesson in life of nil admirari, which is far more necessary to social salvation in snob-ridden England than ever it could have been in the Rome of the Cæsars.

On their way back to college, after a stroll round the meadows, they met a very small telegraph boy at the doors of Durham.

'Message for you, sir,' the porter said, touching his hat to Dick; and in great doubt and trepidation, for to him a telegram was a most rare event, Dick took it and opened it.

His face flushed crimson as he read the contents; but he saw in a second the only way out of it was to put the best face on things.

'Why, my father's coming up, too!' he said, turning round to Gillingham. 'He'll arrive tomorrow. I—I must go this moment and hunt up some rooms for him. My sister doesn't say by what train he's coming; but he evidently means to stay, from what she tells me.'

'One good turn deserves another,' Gillingham drawled out carelessly. 'I don't mind going round with you and having another hunt. I should think that second set we saw round the corner would just about suit him.'

The second set had been rated at seven guineas a week. Dick was weak enough to colour again.

'Oh no,' he answered hurriedly. 'I—I'd prefer to go alone. Of course, I shall want some much cheaper place than that. I think I can get the kind of thing I require in Grove Street.'

'As you will,' Gillingham answered lightly, nodding a brisk farewell, and turning back into quad. 'Far be it from me to inflict my company unwillingly on any gentleman anywhere. I'm all for Auberon Herbert and pure individualism. I say you, Faussett, here's a game;' and he walked mysteriously round the corner by the Warden's Lodgings. He dropped his voice to a whisper: 'The Head of the Plantagenets is coming up tomorrow to visit the Prince of the Blood—fact! I give you my word for it. So we'll have an opportunity at last of finding out who the dickens the fellow is, and where on earth he inherited the proud name of Plantagenet from.'

'There were some Plantagenets at Leeds, no; I think it was Sheffield,' Faussett put in, trying to remember. 'Somebody was saying to me the other day this man might be related to them. The family's extinct, and left a lot of money.'

'Then they can't have anything to do with our Prince of the Blood,' Gillingham answered carelessly; 'for he isn't a bit extinct, but alive and kicking: and he hasn't got a crooked sixpence in the world to bless himself with. He lives on cold tea and Huntley and Palmer's biscuits. But he's not a bad sort, either, when you come to know him; but you've got to know him first, as the poet observes: and he's really a fearful swell at the history of the Plantagenets.'

Dick passed a troubled night. Terrible possibilities loomed vague before him. Next day he was down at the first two trains by which he thought it at all possible his father might arrive; and his vigilance was rewarded by finding Mr. Plantagenet delivered by the second. The Head of the House was considerably surprised, and not a little disappointed, when he saw his son and heir awaiting him on the platform.

'What, you here, Dick!' he cried. 'Why, I wanted to surprise you. I intended to take my modest room for the night at the same hotel at which you stopped, the Saracen's Head, if I recollect the name aright, and then to drop in upon you quite unexpectedly about lunch-time.'

'Maud telegraphed to me that you were coming, father,' Dick answered, taking his hand, it must be acknowledged, a trifle less warmly than filial feeling might have dictated. Then his face grew fiery red. 'But I've engaged rooms for you,' he went on, 'not at an inn, on purpose. I hope, father, for your own sake, as well as for mine, while you're here in Oxford you won't even so much as enter one.'

It was a hard thing to have to say; but, for very shame's sake, Dick felt he must muster up courage to say it.

As for Mr. Plantagenet himself, poor old sot that he was, a touch of manly pride brought the colour just for once to his own swollen cheek.

'I hope, Richard,' he said, drawing himself up very erect, for he had a fine carriage still, in spite of all his degradation, 'I hope I have sufficient sense of what becomes a gentleman, in a society of gentlemen, to think of doing anything that would I disgrace myself, or disgrace my son, or disgrace my name, or my literary reputation, which must be well known to many students of English literature in this University, by any unbecoming act of any description. And I take it hardly, Richard, that my eldest son, for whom I have made such sacrifices', Mr. Plantagenet had used that phrase so often already in the parlour of the White Horse that he had almost come by this time to believe himself there was really some truth in it, 'should greet me with such marked distrust on the very outset of a visit to which I had looked forward with so much pride and pleasure.'

It was quite a dignified speech for Mr. Plantagenet. Dick's, heart was touched by it.

'I beg your pardon, father,' he replied in a very low tone. 'I'm sorry if I've hurt you. But I meant no rudeness. I've engaged pleasant lodgings for you in a very nice street, and I'm sure I'll do everything in my power to make your visit a happy one.'

As he spoke he almost believed his father would rise for once to the height of the circumstances, and behave himself circumspectly with decorum and dignity during his few days at Oxford.

To do Mr. Plantagenet justice, indeed, he tried very hard to keep straight for once, and during all his stay he never even entered the doors of a hotel or public-house. Nay, more; in Dick's own rooms, as Dick noticed with pleasure, he was circumspect in his drinking. It flattered his vanity and his social pretensions to be introduced to his son's friends and to walk at his ease through the grounds of the college. Once more for a day or two Edmund Plantagenet felt himself a gentleman among gentlemen.

Dick kept as close to him as possible, except at lecture hours; and then, as far as he could, he handed him over to the friendly care of Gillespie, who mounted guard in turn, and seemed to enter silently into the spirit of the situation. As much as possible, on the other hand, Dick avoided for those days Gillingham and Faussett's set, whose only wish, he felt sure, would be to draw his father into wild talk about the Plantagenet pedigree, a subject which Dick himself, in spite of his profound faith, had the good sense to keep always most sedulously in the background.

For the first three days Dick was enabled to write nightly and report to Maud that so far all went well, and there were no signs of a catastrophe. But on the fourth day, as ill-luck would have it, Gillingham came round to Faussett's rooms full of a chance discovery he had that moment lighted upon.

'Why, who'd ever believe it?' he cried, all agog. 'This man Plantagenet, who's come up to see his son, the Prince of the Blood, is a decayed writer, a man of letters of the Alaric Watts and Leigh Hunt period, not unheard of in his day as an inflated essayist. I know a lot of his stuff by heart, Hazlitt-and-water sort of style; De Quincey gone mad, with a touch of Bulwer. Learnt it when I was a boy, and we lived at Constantinople. He's the man who used to gush under the name of Barry Neville!'

'How did you find it out?' Faussett inquired, all eagerness.

'Why, I happened to turn out a "Dictionary of Pseudonyms" at the Union just now, in search of somebody else; and there the name Plantagenet caught my eye by chance. So of course I read, and, looking closer, I found this fact about the old man and his origin. It's extremely interesting. So, to make quite sure, I boarded Plantagenet five minutes ago with the point-blank question. "Hullo,

Prince," said I, "I see your father's Barry Neville, the writer." He coloured up to his eyes, as he does, it's a charming girlish trick of his; but he admitted the impeachment. There! he's crossing the quad now. I wonder what the dickens he's done with his governor!'

'I'll run up to his rooms and see,' Faussett answered, laughing. 'He keeps the old fellow pretty close, in cotton wool, so to speak. Won't trust him out alone, and sets Gillespie to watch him. But an Exeter man tells me he's seen the same figure down at a place called Chiddingwick, where he lives, in Surrey; and according to him, he's a rare old buffer. I'll go and make his acquaintance, now his R'yal Highness has gone off unattended to lecture; we'll have some sport out of him.'

And he disappeared, brimming over, up the steps of the New Buildings.

All that afternoon, in fact, Richard noticed for himself that some change had come over his father's spirit. Mr. Plantagenet was more silent, and yet even more grandiose and regal than ever. He hadn't been drinking, thank Heaven, not quite so bad as that, for Dick knew only too well the signs of drink in his father's face and his father's actions; but he had altered in demeanour, somehow, and was puffed up with personal dignity even more markedly than usual. He sat in, and talked a great deal about the grand days of his youth, and he dwelt so much upon the past glories of Lady Postlethwaite's salon and the people he used to meet there that Dick began to wonder what on earth it portended.

'You'll come round to my rooms, father, after Hall?' he asked at last, as Mr. Plantagenet rose to leave just before evening chapel. 'Gillespie'll be here, and one or two other fellows.'

Mr. Plantagenet smiled dubiously.

'No, no, my boy,' he answered in his lightest and airiest manner. 'You must excuse me. This evening, you must really excuse me. To tell you the truth, Richard', with profound importance, 'I have an engagement elsewhere.'

'An engagement, father! You have an engagement! And in Oxford, too,' Dick faltered out. 'Why, how on earth can you have managed to pick up an engagement?'

Mr. Plantagenet drew himself up as he was wont to do for the beginning of a quadrille, and, assuming an air of offended dignity, replied with much hauteur:

'I am not in the habit, Richard, of accounting for my engagements, good, bad, or indifferent, to my own children. I am of age, I fancy. Finding myself here at Oxford in a congenial society, in the society to which I may venture to say I was brought up, and of which, but for unfortunate circumstances, I ought always to have made a brilliant member, finding myself here in my natural surroundings, I repeat, I have, of course, picked up, as you coarsely put it, a few private acquaintances on my own account. I'm not so entirely dependent as you suppose upon you, Richard, for my introduction to Oxford society. My own personal qualities and characteristics, I hope, go a little way, at least, towards securing me respect and consideration in whatever social surroundings I may happen to be mixing.'

And Mr. Plantagenet shook out a clean white cambric pocket-handkerchief ostentatiously, to wipe his eyes, in which a slight dew was supposed to have insensibly collected at the thought of Richard's unfilial depreciation of his qualities and opportunities.

'I'm sorry I've offended you, father,' Dick answered hastily. 'I'm sure I didn't mean to. But I do hope, I do hope, if you'll allow me to say so, you're not going round to spend the evening, at any other undergraduate's rooms, not at Gillingham's or Faussett's.'

Mr. Plantagenet shuffled uneasily: in point of fact, he looked very much as he had been wont to look in days gone by, when the landlady at the White Horse inquired of him now and again how soon he intended to settle his little account for brandy-and-sodas.

'I choose my own acquaintances, Richard,' he answered, with as much dignity as he could easily command. I don't permit myself to be dictated to in matters like this by my own children. Your neighbour Mr. Faussett appears to me a very intelligent and gentlemanly young man: a young man such as I was accustomed to associate with myself in my own early days, before I married your poor dear mother: not like your set, Richard, who are far from being what I myself consider thoroughly gentlemanly. Mere professional young men, your set, my dear boy: very worthy, no doubt, and hard-working, and respectable, like this excellent Gillespie; but not with that cachet, that indefinable something, that invisible hall-mark of true blood and breeding, that I observe with pleasure in your neighbour Faussett. It's not your fault, my poor boy: I recognise freely that it's not your fault. You take after your mother. She's a dear good soul, your mother', pocket-handkerchief lightly applied again, 'but she's not a Plantagenet, Richard: she's not a Planta-genet.'

And with this parting shot neatly delivered point-blank at Dick's crimson face, the offended father sailed majestically out of the room and strode down the staircase.

Dick's cheek was hot and red with mingled pride and annoyance; but he answered nothing. Far be it from him to correct or rebuke by word or deed the living Head of the House of Plantagenet.

'I hope to God,' he thought to himself piteously, 'Faussett hasn't asked him on purpose to try and make an exhibition of him. But what on earth else can he have wanted to ask him for, I wonder?'

At that very same moment Faussett was stopping Trevor Gillingham in the Chapel Quad with a characteristic invitation for a wine-party that evening.

'Drop in and have a glass of claret with me after Hall, Gillingham,' he said, laughing. 'I've got a guest coming to-night. I've asked Plantagenet's father round to my rooms at eight. He'll be in splendid form. He's awfully amusing when he talks at his ease, I'm told. Do come and give us one of your rousing recitations. I want to make things as lively as I can, you know.'

Gillingham smiled the tolerant smile of the Born Poet.

'All right, my dear boy,' he answered. 'I'll come. It'll be stock-in-trade to me, no doubt, for an unborn drama. Though Plantagenet's not half a bad sort of fellow, after all, when you come to know him, in spite of his smugging. Still, I'll come, and look on: an experience, of course, is always an experience. The poet's life must necessarily be made up of infinite experiences. Do you think Shakespeare always kept to the beaten path of humanity? A poet can't afford it. He must see some good, of a sort, in everything; for he must see in it at least material for a tragedy or a comedy.'

With which comfortable assurance to salve his poetical conscience the Born Bard strolled off, in cap and gown, with an easy lounging gait, to evening chapel.

Mr. Plantagenet for a song! Mr. Plantagenet for a song! Hurrah for the Plantagenet!'

The table rang with the knocking of knuckles and the low cries of half-tipsy boys as the half-tipsy old man rose solemnly before them, and proceeded to deliver himself in his earliest style of his famous carol of 'Bet, the Bagman's Daughter.' He was certainly in excellent feather. Standing tall and erect, with the enlivenment of the wine to support him for the moment; all the creases smoothed out of his back, and half the wrinkles out of his brow; even his coarse, bloated face softened a little by the unusual society in which he found himself, Mr. Plantagenet sang his song as he had never sung it at the White Horse at Chiddingwick, with great verve, go, and vigour. He half blushed once or twice, at least, he would have blushed if his cheeks were capable of getting much redder, when he came to the most doubtful verses of that very doubtful composition; but the lads beside him only clapped the harder, and cried, 'Bravo!' 'Jolly good song!' and 'Well done, Mr. Plantagenet!' so he kept through bravely to the very end, singing as he had never sung before since he was a promising young man of eight-and-twenty, the lion of Lady Postlethwaite's delightful entertainments.

As he sat down a perfect chorus of applause rent the air, and Faussett, anxious not to let so good an opportunity slip by, took occasion to fill Mr. Plantagenet's glass twice over in succession: once during the course of the boisterous song, and once at the end to reward his efforts.

The old man had been unusually circumspect, for him, at first, for he vaguely suspected in his own mind that Faussett might have asked him there on purpose to make him drunk; and though there was nothing he liked better than an opportunity of attaining that supreme end of his existence at somebody else's expense, he had still some faint sense of self-respect left, lingering somewhere in some unsuspected back corner of his poor old ruined personality, which made him loath to exhibit his shame and degradation before so many well-bred and gentlemanly young Oxonians. But as time wore on, and the lads applauded all his jokes and songs and stories to the echo, Mr. Plantagenet's heart began by degrees to soften. He was wronging these ingenuous and eminently companionable young fellows. He was over-suspicious in supposing they wanted to make fun of him or to get fun out of him. They had been naturally attracted and pleased by his marked social qualities and characteristics. They recognised in him, under all disguises of capricious fortune, a gentleman and a Plantagenet. He helped himself complacently to another glass of sherry. He held up the golden liquid and glanced askance at the light through it, then he took a delicate sip and rolled it on his palate appreciatively.

It was not very good sherry. An Oxford wine merchant's thirty-six shilling stuff (for undergraduate consumption) can hardly be regarded as a prime brand of Spanish vintage; but it was, at least, much better than Mr. Plantagenet had been in the habit of tasting for many years past, and perhaps his palate was hardly capable any longer of distinguishing between the nicer flavours of hocks or clarets. He put his glass down with rising enthusiasm.

'Excellent Amontillado!' he said, pursing up his lips with the air of a distinguished connoisseur. 'Excellent Amontillado! It's a very long time since I tasted any better.'

Which was perfectly true, as far as it went, though not exactly in the nature of a high testimonial to the character of the wine.

Now, nothing pleases a boy of twenty, posing as a man, so much as to praise his port and sherry. Knowing nothing about the subject himself, and inwardly conscious of his own exceeding ignorance, he accepts the verdict of anybody who ventures upon having an opinion with the same easy readiness as the crowd at the Academy accepts the judgment of anyone present who says aloud, with dogmatic certainty, that any picture in the place is well or ill painted.

'It is good sherry,' Faussett repeated, much mollified. 'Have another glass!'

Mr. Plantagenet assented, and leaned back in an easy-chair as being the safest place from which to deliver at ease his aesthetic judgments for the remainder of that evening. For the wine-party was beginning now to arrive at the boisterous stage. There were more songs to follow, not all of them printable; and there was loud, dull laughter, and there was childish pulling of bonbon crackers, and still more childish shying of oranges at one another's heads across the centre table. The fun was waxing fast and furious. Mr. Plantagenet at the same time was waxing hilarious.

'Gentlemen,' he said, holding his glass a little obliquely in his right hand, and eyeing it with his head on one side in a very doubtful attitude—'Gentlemen.' And at that formal beginning a hush of expectation fell upon the flushed faces of the noisy lads, ready to laugh at the drunken old man who might have been the father of any one among them.

'Hush, hush, there! Mr. Plantagenet for a speech!' Faussett shouted aloud, drumming his glass on the table.

'Hear, hear!' Gillingham cried, echoing the appeal heartily. 'The Plantagenet for a speech! Give us a speech, Mr. Plantagenet!'

Gillingham was a great deal soberer than any of the others, but he was anxious to make notes internally of this singular phenomenon. The human intellect utterly sunk and degraded by wine and debauchery forms a psychological study well worthy the Born Poet's most attentive consideration. He may need it some day for a Lear or an Othello.

Mr. Plantagenet struggled up manfully upon his shaky legs. 'Gentlemen,' he murmured, in a voice a little thick, to be sure, with drinking, but still preserving that exquisitely clear articulation for which Edmund Plantagenet had always been famous—'Gentlemen, it gives me great pleasure to find myself at last, after a long interval of comparative eclipse, in such exceedingly congenial and delightful society. In fact, I may say in the society of my equals, yes, gentlemen, of my equals. I am not proud; I will put it simply "of my equals." Time was, 'tis true, when the name of Plantagenet would, perhaps, have implied something more than mere equality, but I pass that. To insist upon the former greatness and distinction of one's family is as ill-bred and obtrusive as it is really superfluous. But since we here this evening have now sunk into our anecdotage, I will venture to narrate to you a little anecdote'—here Mr. Plantagenet swayed uneasily from one side to the other, and Gillingham, ever watchful, propped him up from behind with much anxious show of solicitous politeness, 'a little anecdote of a member of my own kith and kin, with whose name you are all doubtless well acquainted. My late relative, Edward Plantagenet, the Black Prince—'

At the mention of this incongruous association, most seriously delivered, such a sudden burst of unanimous laughter broke at once from the whole roomful of unruly boys that Mr. Plantagenet, taken aback, felt himself quite unable to continue his family reminiscences. The roar of amusement stunned and half sobered him. He drew his hand across his forehead with a reflective air, steadied himself on his legs, and, shading his eyes with his hand, looked across the table with a frown at the laughing conspirators. Then a light seemed to dawn upon him spasmodically for a moment; the next, again, it had faded away. He forgot entirely the thread of his story, gazed around him impotently with a bland smile of wonder, and sank back into his chair at last with the offended dignity of hopeless drunkenness. It was a painful and horrible sight. To hide his confusion he filled his glass up once more with the profoundest solemnity, tossed it off at a gulp to prevent spilling it, and glanced round yet again upon the tittering company, as if he expected another round of generous applause to follow his efforts.

'He's drunk now, anyhow—dead drunk,' one of the gentlemanly and congenial young fellows half whispered to Gillingham. 'Let's mix all the heeltaps for him with a little soapsuds, and make him swallow them off out of the washhand basin, shall we?'

Gillingham's taste was revolted by the gross vulgarity of this practical suggestion. 'No, no!' he replied, without attempting to conceal his genuine disgust; 'have you no respect at all for his age and his degradation? Don't you know that a drunken old man is too sacred a thing to be made the common butt of your vulgar ridicule? Dionysus was a great god, a great god in his cups, and even Silenus still retains the respect due to gray hairs. Let him alone, I say; he has lowered himself enough, and more than enough, already, without your trying to lower him any further.'

'Why, you helped in the fun as well as we did,' Westall answered, grumbling. 'You needn't try to go and make yourself out such a saint as all that after it's done and finished, for it was you who got him on his legs to make a fool of himself, anyhow.' 'Shakespeare must have studied his Falstaff at all moments and in all phases,' Gillingham replied oracularly, with his gravest irony; 'but I refuse to believe he ever conspired with a set of young blockheads at the Boar in Eastcheap to mix dregs of sherris sack with beer and soapsuds in a common washhand basin for Green or Marlowe. The Born Poet observes; he does not instigate.'

'Hush, hush!' Faussett cried again. 'Mr. Plantagenet is going to address us. Another speech from the Plantagenet!'

'Hear, hear!' Gillingham echoed as before. 'More experiences, more experiences! Life is wide, and its reflection must be many-sided; we want all experiences harmoniously combined to produce the poet, the philosopher, and the ruler.'

'Gentlemen,' Mr. Plantagenet began afresh, rising feebly to his legs and gazing around upon the assembled little crowd in puzzled bewilderment, 'I'm not quite myself this evening, ladies and gentlemen; my old complaint, my old complaint, gentlemen.' Here he laid his hand pathetically upon his heart, amid a chorus of titters. 'Gentlemen, choose your partners. Bow, and fall into places. Eight bars before beginning, then advance in couples, right, left, down the middle. I'll strike up immediately. My violin, my violin! what have you done with it, gentlemen?'

'Gracious heavens!' Gillingham cried, looking over to Faussett, and hardly more than half whispering; 'why, don't you understand? the man's a dancing-master. He thinks we're his pupils, and he's going to make us dance the lancers!'

'By Jove, so he is!' Faussett exclaimed, delighted at this new development of the situation.

'Let's humour him. Fall into places, and let's have the lancers. Here, Tremenbeere, you be my partner.'

But before they could carry out this ingenious arrangement Mr. Plantagenet had suddenly discovered his mistake, and sat down, or, rather, sank with Gillingham's assistance into his easy-chair, where he sat now once more, blankly smiling a vacuous and impenetrable smile upon the uproarious company.

'Stick him out in the yard!' 'Pour cold water over him!' 'Give him a dose of cayenne!'

'Turn his coat inside out, and send him to find his way home with a label pinned upon him!' shouted a whole chorus of congenial and gentlemanly young fellows in varying voices, with varying suggestions for completing the degradation of the poor drunken old creature.

'No!' Gillingham thundered out in a voice of supreme command; 'do nothing of the sort. You wretched Philistines, you've had your fun out of him; and precious poor fun it is, too, all you, who are not students of human nature. You've got to leave him alone, now, I tell you, and give him time to recover. Here, Faussett, lend me a hand with him; he's sound asleep. Let's put him over here to sleep it off upon the sofa.'

Faussett obeyed without a word, and they laid the old man out at full length on the couch to sleep off his first drowsiness.

'Now draw him a bottle of neat seltzer,' Gillingham went on with a commanding air; 'you've got to get him out of college somehow before twelve o'clock, you know; and it's better for yourselves to get him out sober. There'll be a precious hot row if he goes out so drunk that the porter has to help him, and worse still if the scouts come in and find him here in your rooms tomorrow morning.'

This common-sense argument, though coming from the Born Poet, seemed so far cogent to the half-tipsy lads that they forthwith exerted themselves to the utmost of their power in drawing the seltzer, and to holding it to Mr. Plantagenet's unwilling lips. After a time the old man half woke up again dreamily, and then Gillingham set to work to try a notable experiment.

'Have you ever heard of Barry Neville, Westall?' he asked, looking hard at him.

'Neville? Neville?' Westall murmured, turning the name over dubiously. 'Well, no, I don't think so. Of this college?'

'Of this college!' Gillingham echoed contemptuously. 'Of this college indeed! No, not of this college. The ideas of most Durham men seem to be bounded strictly by the four blessed walls of this particular college! I thought you wouldn't know him; I guessed as much. And yet he had once a European reputation. Barry Neville,' raising his voice so that Mr. Plantagenet should hear him distinctly—'Barry Neville was an able essayist, poet and journalist of the middle period of this present century.'

'Well?' Westall went on inquiringly.

'Well,' Gillingham answered, nodding his head with a mysterious look towards the half-awakened drunkard, who had started up at the sound of that familiar name, 'there he lies over on the sofa.'

This last was murmured below his breath to the other lads, so that Mr. Plantagenet didn't catch it in his further corner.

'I'm going to try the effect of a bit of his own writing upon him to-night,' Gillingham continued quietly. 'I'm going to see whether it'll rouse him, or whether he'll even recognise it. Here, you men, stop your row. I'm thinking of giving you a little recitation.'

'Hear, hear!' Faussett cried, languidly interested in the strange experiment. 'Gillingham for a recitation! You know, Mr. Plantagenet, our friend Gillingham, the Born Poet, is celebrated as one of the finest and most versatile reciters in all England.'

'What's he going to give us?' Mr. Plantagenet asked, endeavouring to seem quite wide-awake, and to assume a carefully critical attitude.

'A piece from a forgotten author,' Gillingham answered with quiet dignity. And then, mounting upon the table, and ensuring silence by a look or two flung with impartial aim at the heads of all those who still continued to talk or giggle, he began, in his clear, loud, sonorous voice, to deliver with very effective rhetoric a flashy show-piece, which he had long known by heart among his immense repertory, from the 'Collected Essays of Barry Neville.'

'But of all the terrible downfalls which this world encloses for the eye of the attentive and observant spectator, what downfall, I ask, can be more terrible or more ghastly than that inevitable decadence from the golden hopes and aspirations of youth, to the dreary realities and blasted ideals of dishonoured age? For the young man, this prosaic planet floats joyously and lightly down a buoyant atmosphere of purpled clouds; his exuberant fancy gilds the common earth as the dying sunlight gilds the evening waters with broad streets and paths of refulgent glory. To the old man, the sun itself has faded slowly, but hopelessly, out of the twilight heavens: dark and murky fogs, risen from behind the shadows of that unknown future, have obscured and disfigured with their dark exhalations the bright imaginings of his joyous springtide: evil habits, begun in the mere rush of youthful spirits, have clung to and clogged the marred wings of his soul, till at last, disheartened, disgraced, unhonoured and unfriended, he drifts gradually onward down the unrelenting stream of the years to that final cataract where all his hopes, alike of time and of eternity, are doomed to be finally wrecked and confounded together in one unutterable and irretrievable ruin.

'"Nay, think not, young man, that, because you are gay and bright and vital to-day, you will find the path of life throughout as smooth and easy as you find it now at the very start or outset of your appointed pilgrimage. Those juicy fruits that stretch so temptingly by the bosky wayside, those golden apples of the Hesperides that hang so lusciously from the bending boughs, those cool draughts that spring so pellucid from yon welling fountain, those fair nymphs that bid you loiter so often among the roses and eglantines of yon shady bowers, all, all, though they smile so innocent and so attractive, are but deceitful allurements to delay your feet and intoxicate your senses, toils to lead you aside from the straight but thorny road of right and duty into the brighter but deadly track of fatal self-indulgence. Yet, above all things, if you would be wise, O youth! shun that sparkling beaker, which the cunning tempter, like Comus in the masque, holds out to you too enticingly to quench your ardent thirst: quaff it not, though it dance and glitter so merrily in the sunlight, for there is death in the cup; it leads you on slowly and surely to the dishonoured grave; it loses you, one after another, health, wealth, and youth, and friends, and children; it covers you with shame, disgrace, and humiliation, and in the end this, this, this is the miserable plight to which it finally reduces what may once have been a man of birth, of learning, of genius, and of reputation."' It was a tawdry bit of cheap rhetoric enough, to be sure, penned by Edmund Plantagenet in his palmiest days, when he still cherished his dream of literary greatness, in feeble imitation of De Quincey's rounded and ornate periods; but delivered as Trevor Gillingham knew how to deliver the merest tinsel, with rolling voice and profound intonations of emotion, it struck even those graceless, half-tipsy undergraduates as a perfect burst of the divinest eloquence. They didn't notice at the moment its cheap effectiveness, its muddled metaphors, its utter vulgarity of idea and expression; they were taken unexpectedly by its vivid separate elements, its false gallop of prose, its quick turns of apostrophe, exhortation and sentimentalism, its tricky outer semblance of poetical phraseology. And Gillingham knew how to make the very best of it: pointing now with his left hand upward to the golden apples of the Hesperides hanging from the imaginary branches of trees overhead; now with his right to one side toward the fair nymphs loitering unperceived in their invisible bowers among the Carlsbad plums; and now again with both together downwards towards the awful abyss that he seemed to behold opening unseen upon the carpet before him. And when at last he reached the weak and tawdry climax, 'this, this is the plight to which it finally reduces a man of genius,' he gave fresh point to the words by turning his forefinger relentlessly and reproachfully toward the very author who wrote them, the now fully-awakened and listening dancing-master.

And Edmund Plantagenet himself? Sitting up, half recumbent, upon the bare little sofa, with bloodshot eyes gazing out straight in front of him, he seemed transfixed and spell-bound by the sudden sound of his own young words coming back to him so unexpectedly across the gulf of blighted hopes and forgotten aspirations. Listening eagerly with strained ears to Gillingham's high and measured, cadences, the old man felt for a moment inspired with a new and strange admiration for his own unrecognised eloquence. The phrases, though he remembered them well, seemed to him far finer than when he first had written them, and so indeed they were, transfigured and reduced to a semblance of higher meaning by the practised reciter's stirring elocution. The reciter had produced a deeper effect than he intended. One minute the old man sat there silent after Gillingham had finished, looking round him defiantly with his bloated red face upon those now sobered boys; then, with an unwonted burst of energy and fire, he cried aloud in a tone of suppressed passion:

'Lads, lads, he says the truth! He says the truth! Every word of it. Do you know who wrote that magnificent passage of English rhetoric he has just repeated to you? Do you know who wrote it? It was me, me, me, the last of the Plantagenets! And he knows it. He's been reciting it now to shame and disgrace me in my blighted old age. But, still, he has done wisely. He thought I was past shaming. Lads, lads, I'm not past it. I remember well when I wrote that passage, and many another as fine, or finer. But that's all gone now, and what am I to-day? A miserable drunken old country dancing-master, that a pack of irreverent Oxford boys ask up to their rooms to make fun of him by getting him to drink himself silly. But when I wrote that passage I was young, and full of hope, and an author, and a gentleman. Yes, boys, a gentleman. I knew all the best men and women of my time, and they thought well of me, and prophesied fair things for me not a few. Ah, yes, you may smile, but I remember to-night how Samuel Taylor Coleridge himself took me once by the hand in those days, and laid his honoured palms on my head, and gave me his blessing. And finely it's been fulfilled!' he added bitterly. 'And finely it's been fulfilled, as you see this evening!'

He rose, steady now and straight as an arrow, shaking his long gray hair fiercely off his forehead, and glaring with angry eyes at Trevor Gillingham. 'Come, come,' he said; 'you've had your fun out, boys; you've seen the humiliation of a ruined old man. You've gloated over the end of somebody better to begin with than any one of you is or ever will be, if you live to be twice as old as Methuselah; and now you may go to your own rooms, and sleep your own silly debauch off at your leisure. I will go, too. I have learned something to-night. I have learned that Edmund Plantagenet's spirit isn't as wholly dead or as broken as you thought it, and as he thought it, and I'm glad for my own sake, Mr. Gillingham, to have learned it. Good-night, and good-bye to you all, young gentlemen. You won't have the chance to mock an old man's shame again, if I can help it. But go on as you've begun, go on as you've begun, my fine fellows, and your end will be ten thousand times worse than mine is. Why,' with a burst of withering indignation, 'when I was your age, you soulless, senseless, tipsy young reprobates, I'd have had too much sense of shame, to get my passing amusement out of the pitiable degradation of a man who might fairly have been my grandfather!'

He walked to the door, upright, without flinching, and turned the handle, as sober for the minute as if he hadn't tasted a single glass of sherry. Gillingham, thoroughly frightened now, tried his best to stop him.

'I'm sorry I've hurt your feelings, Mr. Plantagenet,' he stammered out, conscious even as he spoke how weak and thin were his own excuses by the side of the old man's newly-quickened indignation. 'I—I didn't mean to offend you. I wanted to see, to see what effect a few of your own powerful words and periods would produce upon you, falling so unexpectedly on your ear in a society where you probably imagined you had never been heard of. I—I intended it merely as a delicate compliment.'

Edmund Plantagenet answered him never a word, but with a profound bow that had nothing of the dancing-master in it, but a great deal of the angry courtesy of fifty years since, shut the door sternly in his face, and turned to descend the winding stone staircase.

'I'm afraid we've done it now, Faussett,' Trevor Gillingham exclaimed, with a very white face, turning round to the awed and silent company. 'I hope to goodness he won't go and do himself some mischief!'

'Too drunk for that,' Faussett answered carelessly. 'By the time he's got downstairs he'll forget all about it, and reel home to his lodgings as well as he can; he'll never remember a word to-morrow morning.'

A minute later the door opened with a slight knock, and Richard Plantagenet entered, pale and trembling.

'My father,' he cried, looking about the room with a restless glance—'what have you done with my father? I heard his voice as I passed below your windows outside college a minute ago. Where's he gone, Gillingham? What's he been doing in these rooms with you?'

'Mr. Plantagenet has been spending the evening as my guest,' Faussett answered, trying to look as unconcerned as possible; 'but he's just now left, and I believe he's gone home to his own lodgings.'

Dick drew back in horror. He knew from the sound of his father's voice something very unwonted and terrible had happened. Though he had not caught a single word, never before had he heard those lips speak out with such real and angry dignity, and he trembled for the result of so strange an adventure. He rushed back to the porter's lodge, for he had taken a stroll outside that evening on purpose, lest he should see his father the laughing-stock of Faussett and his companions.

'For heaven's sake, porter!' he cried with fervour, 'let me out, let me out, let me out, or there may be murder!'

'Very sorry, sir,' the porter answered with official calmness; the clock's gone eleven. Can't allow you out now without leave from the Dean, sir.'

'Then Heaven save him!' Richard cried, wringing his hands in helpless terror; 'for if he goes out alone like that, God only knows what may become of him!'

'If you mean the elderly gentleman from Mr. Faussett's rooms, sir,' the porter answered cheerfully, 'he seemed to me to walk out quite soberlike and straight, as far as I could see, sir.'

But Dick turned and rushed wildly to his own rooms in the Back Quad, in an agony of suspense for his father's safety.

CHAPTER XII - TRAGEDY WINS

Mr. Plantagenet had missed his son by walking through the archway of the Fellows' Quad, instead of through the Brew House. He emerged from the college by the big front gate. The High Street was lighted and crowded; so he preferred to turn down the dark lanes and alleys at the back of Christ Church, till he came out upon St. Aldate's and the road to the river. Somewhat sobered as he still was by the unwonted excitement of that curious episode, he found the sherry once more beginning to gain the upper hand; it was hard for him to walk erect and straight along the pavement of St. Aldate's, where a few small shops still stood open, for it was Saturday night, and a few people still loitered about in little knots at the corners. With an effort, however, he managed to maintain the perpendicular till he reached Folly Bridge; then he turned in at the wicket that leads down from the main road to the little tow-path along the dark and silent bank of the swollen Isis.

But if Edmund Plantagenet's legs were a trifle unsteady, his heart was all afire with wrath and remorse at this dramatic interlude. For the first time in so many years he began to think bitterly to himself of his wasted opportunities and ruined talents. Such as they were, he had really and truly wasted them; and though perhaps, after all, they were never much to boast of, time had been when Edmund Plantagenet thought highly indeed of them. Nay, in his heart of hearts the broken old dancing-master thought highly of them still, in spite of everything during all those long years. There were nights when he lay awake sobering, on his hard bed at home, and repeated lovingly to himself the 'Stanzas to Evelina' which he had contributed ages ago to the 'Book of Beauty,' or the 'Lines on the Death of Wordsworth' which he printed at the time in the Yorkshire Magazine, with a profound conviction that they contained, after all, some of the really most beautiful and least appreciated poetry in the English language. As a rule, Mr. Plantagenet was fairly contented with himself and his relics of character; it was society, harsh, unfeeling, stupid society, that he blamed most of all for his misfortunes and failures. Still, to every one of us there come now and then moments of genuine self-revelation, when the clouds of egotism and perverse misrepresentation, through which we usually behold our own personality in a glorified halo, fade away before the piercing light of truer introspective analysis, forced suddenly upon us by some disillusioning incident or accident of the moment; and then, for one brief flash, we have the misery and agony of really seeing ourselves as others see us. Such days may Heaven keep kindly away from all of us! Such a day Edmund Plantagenet had now drearily fallen upon. He wandered wildly down the dark bank toward Iffley lasher, his whole soul within him stirred and upheaved with volcanic energy by the shame and disgrace of that evening's degradation. The less often a man suffers from these bruts of self-humiliation, the more terrible is their outburst when they finally do arrive to him. Edmund Plantagenet, loathing and despising his present self, by contrast with that younger and idealized image which had perhaps never really existed at all, stumbled in darkness and despair along that narrow path, between the flooded river on one side and the fence that enclosed the damp water-meadows on the other, still more than half drunk, and utterly careless where he went or what on earth might happen to him.

The river in parts had overflowed its banks, and the towing-path for some yards together was often under water. But Mr. Plantagenet, never pausing, walked, slipped, and staggered through the slush and mud, very treacherous under foot, knowing nothing, heeding nothing, save that the coolness about his ankles seemed to revive him a little and to sober his head as he went floundering through it. By-and-by he reached the Long Bridges, a range of frail planks with wooden side-rails, that lead the tow-path across two or three broad stretches of back-water from the Isis. He straggled across somehow, looking down every now and then into the swirling water, where the stars were just reflected in quick flashing eddies, while all the rest about looked black as night, but, oh! so cool and inviting to his fevered forehead. So he wandered on, fiercely remorseful within, burning hot without, till he came abreast of a row of old pollard-willows, close beside the edge of the little offshoot at Iffley lasher. The bank was damp, but he sat down upon it all the same, and grew half drowsy as he sat with the mingled effects of wine and indignation.

After awhile he rose, and stumbled on across a bend of the meadows till he reached the river. Just there the bank was very slippery and treacherous. Even a sober man could hardly have kept his footing on it in so dark a night. 'One false step,' Edmund Plantagenet thought to himself with wild despair, 'and there would be an end of all this fooling. One false step, and splash! A man may slip any day. No suicide in tumbling into a swollen river of a moonless night when the bank's all flooded.'

Still, on and on he walked, having staggered now far, far below Iffley, and away towards the neighbourhood of Sandford lasher. Slippery bank all the distance, and head growing dizzier and dizzier each moment with cold and wet, as well as wine and anger.

At last, of a sudden, a dull splash in the river! Bargemen, come up late in the evening from Abingdon, and laid by now for the night under shelter of the willows on the opposite side two hundred yards down, heard the noise distinctly. Smoking their pipes on deck very late, it being a fine evening, one says to the other:

'Sounds precious like a man, Bill!'

Bill, philosophically taking a long pull, answers calmly at the end:

'More liker a cow, Tom. None of our business, anyhow. Get five bob, mayhap, for bringin' in the body. Hook it up easy enough to-morrow mornin?

Next morning, sure enough, a body might be seen entangled among the reeds under the steep mud-bank on the Berkshire shore. Bill, taking it in tow and bringing it up to Oxford, got five shillings from the county for his lucky discovery. At the inquest, thought it wise, however, to omit mentioning the splash heard on deck overnight, or that queer little episode of philosophical conversation.

The coroner's jury, for that end empanelled, attentively considering the circumstances which surrounded the last end of Edmund Plantagenet, late of Chiddingwick, Surrey, had more especially to inquire into the question whether or not deceased at the time he met with his sudden death was perfectly sober. Deceased, it seemed, was father of Mr. Richard Plantagenet, of Durham College, who identified the body. On the night of the accident the unfortunate gentleman had dined at his own lodgings in Grove Street, and afterwards went round to take a glass of wine at Mr. T. M. Faussett's rooms in Durham. Mr. Faussett testified that deceased when he left loose rooms was perfectly sober. Mr. Trevor Gillingham, with, the other undergraduates and the college porter, unanimously bore witness to the same effect. Persons in St. Aldate's who had seen deceased on his way to Folly Bridge corroborated this evidence as to sobriety of demeanour. Deceased, though apparently preoccupied, walked as straight as an arrow. On the whole, the coroner considered, all the circumstances seemed to show that Mr. Edmund Plantagenet, who was not a man given to early hours, had strolled off for an evening walk by the river bank to cool himself after dinner, and had slipped and fallen, being a heavy man, owing to the flooded and dangerous state of the tow-path. Jury returned a verdict in accordance with the evidence, accidental death, with a rider suggesting that the Conservators should widen and extend the tow-path.

But Trevor Gillingham, meeting Faussett in quad after Hall that evening, observed to him confidentially in a very low voice:

'By Jove, old man, we've had a precious narrow squeak of it! I only hope the others will be discreetly silent. We might all have got sent down in a lump together for our parts in this curious little family drama. But all's well that end's well, as the Immortal One has it. Might make a capital scene, don't you know, some day—in one of my future tragedies.'

CHAPTER XIII - AN UNEXPECTED VISITOR

His father's death put Dick at once in a very different position from the one he had previously occupied. It was a family revolution. And on the very evening of the funeral, that poor shabby funeral, Dick began then and there to think the future over.

Poor people have to manage things very differently from rich ones; and when Edmund Plantagenet was laid to rest at last in the Oxford cemetery, no member of the family save, Dick himself was there to assist at the final ceremony. Only Gillespie accompanied him to the side of the grave out of all the college; but when they reached the chapel, they found Gillingham standing there hatless before them—urged, no doubt, by some late grain of remorse for his own prime part in this domestic drama; or was it only perhaps by a strong desire to see the last act of his tragedy played out to its bitter climax? After the ceremony he left hurriedly at once in the opposite direction. The two friends walked home alone in profound silence. That evening Gillespie came up to Dick's rooms to bear him company in his trouble. Dick was deeply depressed. After awhile he grew confidential, and explained to his friend the full gravity of the crisis. For Mr. Plantagenet, after all, poor weak sot though he was, had been for many years the chief bread-winner of the family. Dick and Maud, to be sure, had done their best to eke out the housekeeping, expenses, and to aid the younger children as far as possible; but, still, it was the father on whose earnings they all as a family had depended throughout for rent and food and clothing. Only Maud and Dick were independent in any way; Mrs. Plantagenet and the little ones owed everything to the father. He had been a personage at Chiddingwick, a character in his way, and Chiddingwick for some strange reason had always been proud of him. Even 'carriage company' sent their children to learn of him at the White Horse, just because he was 'old Plantagenet,' and a certain shadowy sentiment attached to his name and personality. Broken reprobate as he was, the halo of past greatness followed him down through life to the lowest depths of degradation and penury.

But now that his father was dead, Dick began to realize for the first time how far the whole family had been dependent for support upon the old man's profession. Little as he had earned, indeed, that little had been bread-and-butter to his wife and children. And now that Dick came to face the problem before him like a man, he saw only too plainly that he himself must fill the place Mr. Plantagenet had vacated. It was a terrible fate, but he saw no way out of it. At one deadly blow all his hopes for the future were dashed utterly to the ground. Much as he hated to think it, he saw at once it was now his imperative duty to go down from Oxford. He must do something-without delay to earn a livelihood somehow for his mother and sisters. He couldn't go on living there in comparative luxury while the rest of his family starved, or declined on the tender mercies of the Chiddingwick workhouse.

Gradually, bit by bit, he confided all this, broken-hearted, to Gillespie. There were no secrets between them now; for the facts as to poor Mr. Plantagenet's pitiable profession had come out fully at the inquest, and all Oxford knew that night that Plantagenet of Durham, the clever and rising history man, who was considered safe for the Marquis of Lothian's Essay, was, after all, but the son of a country dancing-master. So Dick, with a crimson face, putting his pride in his pocket, announced to his friend the one plan for the future that now seemed to him feasible—to return at once to Chiddingwick and take up his father's place, so as to keep together the clientele. Clearly he must do something to make money without delay; and that sad resolve was the only device he could think of on the spur of the moment.

'Wouldn't it be better to try for a schoolmaster-ship?' Gillespie suggested cautiously. He had the foresight of his countrymen. 'That wouldn't so much unclass you in the end as the other. You haven't a degree, of course, and the want of one would naturally tell against you. But you might get a vacant place in some preparatory school—though the pay, of course, would be something dreadfully trivial.'

'That's just it,' Dick answered, bursting with shame and misery, but facing it out like a man. 'Gillespie, you're kindness itself, such a dear, good fellow!—and I could say things to you I couldn't say to anybody else on earth that I know of, except my own family. But even to you I can't bear to say what must be said sooner or later. You see, for my mother's sake, for my sisters', for my brothers', I must do whatever enables me to make most money. I must pocket my pride, and I've got a great deal, ever so much too much, but I must pocket it all the same, and think only of what's best in the end for the family. Now, I should hate the dancing, oh, my dear, dear fellow, I can't tell you how I should hate it! But it's the one thing by which I could certainly earn most money. There's a good connection there at Chiddingwiok, and it's all in the hands of the family.

People would support me because I was my father's son. If I went home at once, before anybody else came to the town to fill the empty place, I could keep the connection together; and as I wouldn't spend any money, well, in the ways my poor father often spent it, I should easily earn enough to keep myself and the children. It'll break my heart to do it, oh, it'll break my heart!—for I'm a very proud man; but I see no way out of it. And I, who hoped to build up again by legitimate means the fortunes of the Plantagenets!'

Gillespie was endowed with a sound amount of good Scotch common-sense. He looked at things more soberly.

'If I were you,' he said in a tone that seemed to calm Dick's nerves, 'even at the risk of letting the golden opportunity slip, I'd do nothing rashly. A step down in the social scale is easy enough to take; but, once taken, we all know it's very hard to recover. Have you mentioned this plan of yours to your mother or sister?'

'I wrote to Maud about it this, evening,' Dick answered sadly, 'and I told her I might possibly have to make this sacrifice.'

Gillespie paused and reflected. After a minute's consideration, he drew his pipe from his mouth and shook out the ashes.

'If I were you,' he said again, in a very decided voice, 'I'd let the thing hang a bit. Why shouldn't you run down to Chiddingwick tomorrow and talk matters over with your people? It costs money, I know; and just at present I can understand every penny's a penny to you. But I've a profound respect for the opinions of one's women in all these questions. They look more at the social side, I'll admit, than men; yet they often see things more clearly and intelligently, for all that, than we do. They've got such insight. If they demand this sacrifice of you, I suppose you must make it; but if, as I expect, they refuse to sanction it, why, then, you must try to find some other way out of it.'

Gillespie's advice fell in exactly with Dick's own ideas; for not only did he wish to see his mother and Maud, but also he was anxious to meet Mary Tudor again and explain to her with regret that the engagement which had never existed at all between them must now be ended. So he decided to take his friend's advice at once, and start off by the first train in the morning to Chiddingwick.

He went next day. Gillespie breakfasted with him, and remained when he left in quiet possession of the armchair by the fireside. He took up a book, the third volume of Mommsen, and sat on and smoked, without thinking of the time, filling up the interval till his eleven o'clock lecture. For at eleven the Senior Tutor lectured on Plato's 'Republic.' Just as the clock struck ten, a hurried knock at the door aroused Gillespie's attention.

'Come in!' he said quickly, taking his pipe from his mouth.

The door opened with a timid movement, standing a quarter ajar, and a pale face peeped in with manifest indecision.

'A lady!' Gillespie said to himself, and instinctively knocked the unconsumed tobacco out of his short clay pipe as he rose to greet her.

'Oh, I beg your pardon,' a small voice said, in very frightened accents. 'I think I must be mistaken. I wanted Mr. Richard Plantagenet's rooms. Can you kindly direct me to them?'

'These are Mr. Plantagenet's rooms,' Gillespie answered, as gently as a woman himself, for he saw the girl was slight, and tired, and delicate, and dressed in deep mourning of the simplest description. 'He left me here in possession when he went out this morning, and I've been sitting ever since in them.'

The slight girl came in a step or two with evident hesitation.

'Will he be long gone?' she asked tremulously. 'Perhaps he's at lecture. I must sit down and wait for him.'

Gillespie motioned her into a chair, and instinctively pulled a few things straight in the room to receive a lady.

'Well, to tell you the truth,' he said, 'Plantagenet's gone down this morning to Chiddingwick. I—I beg your pardon, but I suppose you're his sister.'

Maud let herself drop into the chair he set for her, with a despondent gesture.

'Gone to Chiddingwick! Oh, how unfortunate!' she cried, looking puzzled. 'What am I ever to do? This is really dreadful!'

And, indeed, the situation was sufficiently embarrassing; for she had run up in haste, on the spur of the moment, when she received Dick's letter threatening instant return, without any more money than would pay her fare one way, trusting to Dick's purse to frank her back again. But she didn't mention these facts, of course, to the young man in Dick's rooms, with the blue-and-white boating jacket, who sat and looked hard at her with profound admiration, reflecting to himself, meanwhile, how very odd it was of Plantagenet never to have given him to understand that his sister was beautiful! For Maud was always beautiful, in a certain delicate, slender, shrinking fashion, though she had lots of character; and her eyes, red with tears, and her simple little black dress, instead of spoiling her looks, somehow served to accentuate the peculiar charms of her beauty.

She sat there a minute or two, wondering what on earth to do, while Gillespie stood by in respectful silence. At last she spoke.

'Yes, I'm his sister,' she said simply, raising her face with a timid glance towards the strange young man. 'Did Dick tell you when he was coming back? I'm afraid I must wait for him.'

'I don't think he'll be back till rather late,' Gillespie answered, with sympathy. 'He took his name off Hall. That means to say,' he added in explanation, 'he won't be home to dinner.'

Maud considered for a moment in doubt. This was really serious. Then she spoke once more, rather terrified.

'He won't stop away all night, I suppose?' she asked, turning up her face appealingly to the kindly-featured stranger. For what she could do in that case, in a strange, big town, without a penny in her pocket, she really couldn't imagine.

Gillespie's confident answer reassured her on that head.

'Oh no; he won't stop away,' he replied, 'for he hasn't got leave; and he wouldn't be allowed to sleep out without it. But he mayn't be back, all the same, till quite late at night, perhaps ten or eleven. It would be hardly safe for you, I think, to wait on till then for him. I mean,' he added apologetically, 'it might perhaps be too late to get a train back to Chiddingwick.'

Maud looked down and hesitated. She perused the hearthrug.

'I think,' she said at last, after a very long pause, 'you must be Mr. Gillespie.'

'That's my name,' the young man answered, with an inclination of the head, rather pleased she should have heard of him.

Maud hesitated once more. Then, after a moment, she seemed to make her mind up.

'I'm so glad it's you,' she said simply, with pretty womanly confidence; 'for I know you're Dick's friend, and I dare say you'll have guessed what's brought me up here to-day, even in the midst of our great trouble. Oh, Mr. Gillespie, did he tell you what he wrote last night to me?'

Gillespie gazed down at her. Tears stood in her eyes as she glanced up at him piteously. He thought he had never seen any face before so pathetically pretty.

'Ye—es; he told me,' the young man answered; hardly liking even to acknowledge it. 'He said he thought of going back at once to Chiddingwick, to take up—well, to keep together your poor father's connection.'

With a violent effort Maud held back her tears.

'Yes; that's just what he wrote,' she went on, with downcast eyes, her lips trembling as she said it. Then she turned her face to him yet again.

'But, oh, Mr. Gillespie!' she cried, clasping her hands in her earnestness, 'that's just what he must never, never, never think of!'

'But he tells me it's the only thing—the family has—to live upon,' Gillespie interposed, hesitating.

'Then the family can starve!' Maud cried, with a sudden flash of those tearful eyes. 'We're Plantagenets, and we can bear it. But for Dick to leave Oxford, and spoil all our best hopes for him, oh, Mr. Gillespie, can't you feel it would be too, too dreadful? We could never stand it!'

Gillespie surveyed her from head to foot in admiration of her spirit. Such absolute devotion to the family honour struck a kindred chord in his half-Celtic nature.

'You speak like a Plantagenet,' he, answered very gravely, for he, too, had caught some faint infection of the great Plantagenet myth. 'You deserve to have him stop. You're worthy of such a brother. But don't you think yourself it would be right of him, as he does, to think first of your mother and his sisters and brothers?'

Maud rose and faced him.

'Mr. Gillespie,' she cried, clasping her hands, and looking beautiful as she did so, 'I don't know why I can speak to you so frankly: I suppose it's because you're Dick's friend, and because in this terrible loss which has come upon us so suddenly we stand so much in need of human sympathy. But, oh, it's wrong to say it, of course, yet say it I must; I don't care one penny whether it's right or whether it's wrong; let us starve or not, I dodo want Dick to stop on at Oxford!'

Gillespie regarded her respectfully. Such courage appealed to him.

'Well, I dare say I'm as wrong as you,' he answered frankly; 'but, to tell you the truth, so do I; and I honour you for saying it.'

'Thank you,' Maud cried, letting the tears roll now unchecked, for sympathy overcame her. She fell back again into, her chair. 'Do you know,'-she said unaffectedly, 'we don't care one bit what we do at Chiddingwick; we don't care, not one of us! We'd work our fingers to the bone, even Nellie, who's the youngest, to keep Dick at Oxford. We don't mind if we starve, for we're only the younger ones. But Richard's head of our house now, heir of our name and race; and we were all so proud when he got this Scholarship. We thought he'd be brought up as the chief of the Plantagenets ought to be.' She paused a moment and reflected; then she spoke again. 'To leave Oxford would be bad enough,' she went on, 'and would cost us all sore; it would be a terrible blow to us, though, I suppose, that's inevitable; but to come back to Chiddingwick, and take up my dear father's profession, oh, don't think me undutiful to his memory, Mr. Gillespie, for our father was a man, if you'd known him long ago, before he grew careless, a man we had much to be proud of, but still, well, there! if Dick was to do it, it would break our very hearts for us.'

'I can see it would,' Gillespie answered, glancing away from her gently, for she was crying hard now. His heart warmed to the poor girl. How he wished it had been possible for him to help her effectually!

Maud leaned forward with clasped hands, and spoke still more earnestly. 'Then you'll help me with it?' she said, drawing a sigh. 'You'll work with me to prevent him? I know Dick thinks a great deal of your advice and opinion. He's often told me so. You'll try to persuade him not to leave Oxford, won't you? Or if he leaves, at least not to come back to Chiddingwick?

Oh, do say you will! for Dick's so much influenced by what you think and say. You see, he'll want to do what's best for us, he's always so unselfish. But that's not what we want: you must try and make him neglect us, and think only of himself; for the more he thinks of us, the more unhappy and ashamed and desperate he'll make us; and the more he thinks of himself, why, the better we'll all love him.'

It was a topsy-turvy gospel, but one couldn't help respecting it. Gillespie rose and 'sported the oak,' closed the big outer door, which stands as a sign in all Oxford rooms that the occupant is out, or doesn't wish to be disturbed, and so secures men when reading from casual interruption. He told Maud what he had done; and Maud, who had been brought up too simply to distrust her brother's friend, or to recognise the rules of polite etiquette on such subjects, was grateful to him for the courtesy.

'Now, we must talk this out together,' he said, 'more plainly and practically. It's a business matter: we must discuss it as business. But anyhow, Miss Plantagenet, I'll do my very best to help you in keeping Dick on at Oxford.'

CHAPTER XIV - BREAKING IT OFF

At Chiddingwick, meanwhile, Dick Plantagenet himself had been oddly enough engaged on rather opposite business. When he arrived at the house in the High Street, so long his father's, he found Maud flown, of course, and nobody at home but his mother and little Eleanor. Now, if Maud had been there, being a forcible young person in spite of her frail frame, she would soon have stirred up Mrs. Plantagenet to take her own view of the existing situation. But the widow, always weary with the cares of too large a family for her slender means, and now broken by the suddenness of her husband's death, thus left without Maud's aid, was disposed like Dick himself to take the practical side in this pressing emergency. To her, very naturally, the question of bread-and-cheese for the boys and girls came uppermost in consciousness. And though it was terrible they should have to face that sordid question at such a moment as this, yet that was a painful fate they shared, after all, with the vast majority of their fellow-creatures, who constantly have to consider practical difficulties of daily bread at the very time when their affections have just been most deeply lacerated. The more Dick talked with his mother, indeed, the more did he feel himself how imperative a duty it was for him to resign his dream and return home at once, to do what he could for her and his brothers and sisters. He was a Plantagenet, he reflected, and noblesse oblige. That motto of his race stood him in good stead on all such occasions. If do it he must, then do it he would. A Plantagenet should not be ashamed of earning his livelihood and supporting his family in any honest way, however distasteful. For no matter what trade he might happen to take up, being a Plantagenet himself, ipso facto he ennobled it.

Fired with these sentiments, which, after all, were as proud in their way as Maud's equally strong ones, if not even prouder, Dick went out almost at once to inquire at the White Horse about the possibility of his keeping up the rent of the rooms as his father had paid it; for if the scheme was to be worked no time must be lost over it, so that the lessons might be continuous. He was a capital dancer himself (worse luck!) and a tolerable violinist, and, for the matter of that, Maud could help him with the music; though he shrank, to be sure, from the painful idea that the heiress of the Plantagenets, a born princess of the blood royal of England, should mix herself up any longer with that hateful profession.

Oh, how his soul loathed it! Indeed, on second thoughts he decided 't would be best for Maud to-be set free from the classes for her ordinary music lessons. While his father lived he couldn't have done without Maud; but now the head of the house was gone, never more should she be subjected to that horrid slavery. Enough that one member of the family should give himself up to it for the common good. Maud, poor, delicate, high-strung Maud, should, at least, be exempt.

If he needed any help he would hire an assistant.

The interview at the White Horse was quite satisfactory, too satisfactory by far, Dick thought, for he longed for a decent obstacle; and as soon as it was finished Dick felt the hardest part of his self-sacrifice was yet to come. For he had to give up not only Oxford, but also Mary Tudor. For her own sake he felt he must really do it. He had never asked her to think of him till he got his Scholarship; and it was on the strength of that small success he first ventured to speak to her. Now that Oxford must fade like a delicious dream behind him, he saw clearly his hopes of Mary must needs go with it.

They were never engaged: from first to last Mary had always said so, and Dick had admitted it. But, still, they had come most perilously near it. During the Long Vacation, when Dick had had some coaching to do for matriculation at a neighbouring town, he and Mary, had almost arrived at an understanding with one another. Dick was a gentleman now, he had always been a gentleman, indeed, in everything except the artificial position; and since he went to Oxford he had that as well, and Mary felt there was no longer any barrier of any sort interposed between them. But now all, all must go, and he must say farewell for ever to Mary.

It was hard, very hard; but duty before everything! With a beating heart he mounted the Rectory steps, and for the first time in his life ventured to ask boldly out if he could see Miss Tudor. It would be the last time, too, he thought bitterly to himself, and so it didn't matter.

Mrs. Tradescant was kinder than usual. Mr. Plantagenet's sudden death had softened her heart for the moment towards the family, perhaps even towards Maud herself, that horrid girl who committed the unpardonable offence, to a mother, of being prettier and more ladylike than her own eldest daughter. The lady of the Rectory was in the schoolroom with Mary when Ellen, the housemaid, came in with the unwonted message that Mr. Richard Plantagenet, 'him as has gone up to college at Oxford, ma'am, has called for to see Miss Tudor.'

Mary blushed up to her eyes, and expected Mrs. Tradescant would insist upon going down and seeing Dick with her.

But Mrs. Tradescant had a woman's inkling of what was afoot between the two young people; and now that that horrid old man was dead, and Richard his own master, she really didn't know that it very much mattered. Young Plantagenet was an Oxford man, after all, and might go into the Church, and turn out a very good match in the end for Mary Tudor. So she only looked up and said, with a most unusual smile:

'You'd better run down to him, dear. I dare say you'd like best to see him alone for awhile, after all that's happened.'

Taken aback at such generosity, Mary ran down at once, still blushing violently, to Dick in the drawing-room. She hardly paused for a second at the glass on her way, just to pull her front hair straight and rub her cheek with her hand, quite needlessly, to bring up some colour.

Dick was dressed in black from head to foot, and looked even graver and more solemn than usual. He stretched out both his hands to hers as Mary entered, and took her fingers in his own with a regretful tenderness. Then he looked deep into her eyes for some seconds in silence. His heart was full to bursting. How could he ever break it to her? 'Twas so hard to give up all his dreams for ever. At last he found words.

'Oh, Mary,' he cried, trembling, 'you've heard of all that's happened?'

Mary pressed his hand hard, and answered simply, with a great lump in her throat: 'Yes, Dick dear, I've heard, and all these days long I've lived with you constantly.'

Dick sat down on the sofa and began to tell her all his story. He told her first about his father's death and the things that had followed it; and then he went on to the more immediately practical question of what he was to do for his mother and sisters. His voice trembled as he spoke, for he was very, very fond of her; but he told her all straight out, as a Plantagenet should, without one word of the disgrace he felt it would be. He dwelt only on the absolute necessity of his doing something at once to provide for the family.

'And under these circumstances, Mary,' he said at last, looking down at her with some moisture in his brimming eyes. 'I feel that my duty to you is perfectly plain and clear. I must release you unconditionally from the engagement, which, as we both know, has never existed between us.'

Mary looked at him for a moment as if she hardly took in the full meaning of his words; then, in a. very low and decided voice, she answered clearly: 'But I don't release you, dear Dick, and I shall never release you.'

'But, Mary,' Dick cried, unable to conceal his pleasure at her words, in spite of himself, 'you mustn't think of it, you know. It's, it's quite, quite impossible. In the first place, I shall never be able to marry at all now, or if ever, why, only after years and years, oh, Heaven only knows how many!'

('That's nothing!' Mary sobbed out parenthetically; 'if necessary, I could wait a thousand years for you.')

'And then again,' Dick continued, resolved not to spare himself one solitary drop in his cup of degradation, 'it would never do for you to be engaged—to the local dancing-master. If it comes to that, indeed, I'm sure Mrs. Tradescant wouldn't allow it.'

With a sudden womanly impulse Mary rose all at once and flung herself, sobbing, on her lover's bosom.

'Oh, Dick,' she cried—'dear Dick, I'm proud of you—so proud of you, no matter what you do—prouder now than ever! I think it's just grand of you to be so ready to give up everything for your mother and sisters. You seem to me to think only of them, and of me, and not a word of yourself; and I say it's just beautiful of you. I couldn't be ashamed of you if you sold apples in the street. You'd always be yourself, and I couldn't help being proud of you. And as for Mrs. Tradescant, if she won't let me be engaged to you, why, I'll throw up the place and take another one, if I can get it, or else go without one. But I'm yours now, Dick, and I shall be yours forever.' She threw her arms round his neck, and, for the first time in her life, she raised her lips and kissed him. 'Why, what a wretch I should be,' she cried through her tears, 'if I could dream of giving you up just at the very moment when you most want my help and sympathy! Dick, Dick, dear Dick, we never were engaged till now; but now we are engaged, and you won't argue me out of it!'

Dick led her to a seat. For the next few minutes the conversation was chiefly of an inarticulate character. The type-founder's art has no letters to represent it. Then Dick tried to speak again in the English language. (The rest had been common to the human family.)

'This is very good of you, dearest,' he said, holding her hand tight in his own; 'very, very good and sweet of you! It's just what I might have expected; though I confess, being engaged chiefly in thinking of the thing from the practical standpoint, I didn't expect it, which was awfully dull of me. But we must be practical, practical. I must devote myself in future to my mother and sisters; and you mustn't waste all the best of your life in waiting for me, in waiting for a man who will probably never, never be able to marry you.'

But women, thank God, are profoundly unpractical creatures! Mary looked up in his face through her tears, and made answer solemnly:

'Oh, Dick, you don't know how long I would wait for you! I want to tell you something, dear; to-day I feel I can tell you. I could never have told you before; I wouldn't tell you now if it weren't for all that has happened. Eighteen months ago, when you first spoke to me, I thought to myself: "He's a charming young man, and I like him very much; he's so kind and so clever; but how could I ever marry him? It wouldn't be right; he's the son of the dancing-master." And now to-day, dear Dick, you darling good fellow, if you turn dancing-master yourself, or anything else in the world, if you sweep a crossing, even, I shall be proud of you still; I shall feel prouder of you by far than if you stopped there selfishly in your rooms at Oxford, and never gave a thought to your mother and sisters.'

She paused for a second and looked at him. Then once more she flung her arms round his neck and cried aloud, almost hysterically:

'Oh, Dick, dear Dick, whatever on earth you do, I shall always love you; I shall always be proud of you!'

And when they parted that morning, Richard Plantagenet and Mary Tudor were for the first time in their lives engaged to one another.

That's what always happens when you go to see a girl, conscientiously determined, for her sake, much against the grain, to break things off with her forever. I have been there myself, and I know all about it.

CHAPTER XV - A WILLING PRISONER

At Oxford all that day, Mr. Archibald Gillespie, of Durham College, found himself in a very singular position indeed for an undergraduate of such unquestioned and respectable manners. For he was keeping Maud Plantagenet shut up behind a sported oak in her brother's rooms, and clandestinely supplying her with lunch, tea and dinner.

This somewhat compromising condition of affairs in the third pair left of Back Quad New Buildings had been brought about by a pure concatenation of accidents. When Maud left Chiddingwick that morning, with nothing in her purse, she had trusted to Dick to supply her with the wherewithal for paying her way back again. But as Dick was not at home when she reached his rooms, she had been compelled to wait in for him till he returned from Chiddingwick. For the same reason she was obviously unable to supply herself with food at a hotel or restaurant. Being a Plantagenet, indeed, she would have been far too proud to let Gillespie suspect these facts by overt act or word of hers; but, somehow, he guessed them for himself, and soon found his suspicions confirmed by her very silence.

Now, the scouts, or college servants, have a key of the 'oak,' and can enter men's rooms at any moment without warning beforehand. There was nothing for it, therefore, but for Gillespie to take Dick's scout frankly into his confidence; which he did accordingly. Already he had forgotten his eleven o'clock lecture; Plato's 'Bepublic' had gone to the wall before a pretty face; and now he went outside the door to plot still further treason, and shouted, after the primitive Oxford fashion, for the servant.

'Look here, Robert,' he said, as the scout came up, 'there's a young lady in deep mourning in Mr. Plantagenet's rooms. She's Mr. Plantagenet's sister, and she's come up to see him about this dreadful affair the other day, you understand. But he's gone down home for the morning to Chiddingwick, they've crossed on the road, and he mayn't perhaps be back again till late in the evening. Now, I can see the young lady's got no money about her, she came away hurriedly, and I don't like to offer her any. So I'm going to telegraph to Mr. Plantagenet to come back as soon as he can; but he can't be here for some time yet, anyhow. Of course, the young lady must have something to eat; and I want you to help me with it. Tell the porter who she is, and that she'll probably have to stop here till Mr. Plantagenet comes back. Under the circumstances, nobody will say anything about it. At lunch-time you must take out something quiet and nice in my name from the kitchen, chicken cutlets, and so forth, and serve it to the young lady in Mr. Plantagenet's rooms. When Mr. Plantagenet returns he'll see her out of college.'

As for Robert, standing by obsequious, he grinned from ear to ear at the obvious prospect of a good round tip, and undertook for his part with a very fair grace that the young lady's needs should be properly provided for. Your scout is a person of infinite resource, the most servile of his kind; he scents tips from afar, and would sell his soul to earn one.

Even in this age of enlightenment, however, an Oxford college still retains many traits of the medieval monastery from which it sprang; women are banned in it; and 'twould have been as much as Mr. Robert's place was worth to serve the unknown young lady in Dick Plantagenet's rooms without leave from headquarters. So he made a clean breast of it. Application to the Dean, however, resulted in his obtaining the necessary acquiescence; and Gillespie devoted himself through the rest of that day to making Maud as comfortable as was possible under the circumstances in her brother's rooms till Dick's return from Chiddingwick.

So charitably was he minded, indeed, that he hardly left her at all except at meal-times. Now, in the course of a long day's tête-à-tête two people get to know a wonderful deal of one another, especially if they have mutually sympathetic natures; and before Dick returned that evening to set Maud at liberty, she and Gillespie felt already like old friends together.

Dick didn't get back, as it happened, till long after Hall, and then it was too late for Maud to catch a train back that evening. The reason for the delay was simple; Dick hadn't received Archie Gillespie's telegram till his return from the Rectory. He had stopped there to lunch, at Mrs. Tradescant's request, after his interview with Mary; and for Mary's sake he thought it best to accept the invitation. So the end of it all was that Dick had to find his sister a bed under the friendly roof of a married Fellow of his college, and that before he took her round there, he, she, and Gillespie had a long chat together about the prospects of the situation.

'Mr. Gillespie and I have been talking it over all day, Dick,' Maud said very decidedly; 'and we're both of us of opinion, most distinctly of opinion, that you oughtn't, as a duty to mother and to us, to do anything that'll compel you to take back again the one great forward step you took in coming to Oxford. Mr. Gillespie says rightly, it's easy enough to go down, but not by any means so easy, once you're there, to climb up again.'

'I ought to do whatever makes me earn an immediate income soonest, though, for all your sakes, Maud,' Dick objected stoutly.

'Not at all!' Maud answered with Plantagenet decision, and with wisdom above her years, dictated no doubt by her love and pride in her brother. 'You oughtn't to sacrifice the future to the present.' Then she turned to him quite sharply. 'Did you see Mary Tudor to-day?' she asked, regardless of Gillespie's presence, for she considered him already as an old friend of the family.

The tell-tale colour rushed up fast into Dick's cheek.

'Yes, I did,' he answered, half faltering. 'And she behaved most nobly. She behaved as you'd expect such a girl to behave, Maud. She spoke of it quite beautifully.'

Maud drew back, triumphant. If Mary had been there, she could have thrown her thin arms round her neck and kissed her.

'Well, and she didn't advise you to go and settle at Chiddingwick!' Maud cried with proud confidence.

'She didn't exactly advise me,' Dick answered with some little hesitation; 'but she acquiesced in my doing it; and she said, whatever I did, she'd always love me equally. In point of fact,' Dick added, somewhat sheepishly, 'we never were engaged at all before to-day; but this morning we settled it.'

Maud showed her profound disappointment, nay, almost her contempt, in her speaking face. To say the truth, it's seldom we can any of us see anything both from our own point of view and someone else's as well. Maud could see nothing in all this but profound degradation for Dick, and indirectly for the family, if Dick went back to Chiddingwick; while Mary had only thought how noble and devoted it was of her unselfish lover to give up everything so readily for his mother and sisters.

'I think,' Dick ventured to put in, since Mary's reputation was at stake in Maud's mind, 'she was most—well, pleased that I should be willing to—to make this sacrifice, if I may call it so, because I thought it my duty.'

Maud flung herself on the floor at his side, and held his hand in hers passionately.

'Oh, Dick,' she cried, clinging to him, 'dear Dick! she oughtn't to have thought like that! She oughtn't to have thought of us! She ought to have thought, as I do, of you and your future! If I, who am your sister, am so jealous for your honour, surely she, who's the girl you mean to marry, ought to be ten times more so!'

'So she is,' Dick answered manfully. 'Only, don't you see, Maud, there are different ways of looking at it. She thinks, as I do, that it's best and most imperative to do one's duty first; she would give me up for herself, almost, and wait for me indefinitely, if she thought I could do better so for you and dear mother.'

Maud clung to him passionately still. For it was not to him only she clung, but also to the incarnate honour of the family. 'Oh, Dick,' she cried once more, 'you mustn't do it; you mustn't do it; you'll kill me if you do it! We don't mind starving; that's as easy as anything; but not a second time shall we draggle in the dust of the street the honour of the Plantagenets.'

They sat up late that night, and talked it all over from every side alternately. And the more they talked it over, the more did Gillespie come round to Maud's opinion on the matter. It might be necessary for Dick to leave Oxford, indeed; though even that would be a wrench; but if he left Oxford, it would certainly be well he should take some other work, whatever work turned up, even if less well paid, that would not unclass him.

And before they separated for the night, Maud had wrung this concession at least out of her wavering brother, that he would do nothing decisive before the end of term; and that, meanwhile, he would try to find some more dignified employment in London or elsewhere. Only in the last resort, he promised her, would he return to Chiddingwick, and his father's calling. That should be treated as the final refuge against absolute want. And, indeed, his soul loathed it; he had only contemplated it at first, not for himself, but for his kin, from a stern sense of duty.

Gillespie saw Maud off at the station next morning with Dick. He was carefully dressed, and wore, what was unusual with him, a flower in his button-hole. Maud's last words to him were: 'Now, Mr. Gillespie, remember: I rely upon you to keep Dick from backsliding.'

And Gillespie answered, with a courteous bow to the slim pale little creature who sat in deep mourning on the bare wooden seat of the third-class carriage (South-Eastern pattern): 'You may count upon me, Miss Plantagenet, to carry out your programme.'

As they walked back together silently up the High towards Durham, Gillespie turned with a sudden dart to his friend and broke their joint reverie.

'Is your sister engaged, Dick?' he asked with a somewhat nervous jerk.

'Why, no,' Dick-answered, taken aback, 'at least, not that I ever heard of.'

'I should think she would be soon,' Gillespie retorted meaningly.

'Why so?' Dick inquired in an unsuspecting voice.

'Well, she's very pretty,' Gillespie answered; 'and very clever; and very distinguished-looking.'

'She is pretty,' Dick admitted, unsuspecting as before. No man ever really remembers his own sisters are women. 'But, you see, she never meets any young men at Chiddingwick. There's nobody to make love to her.'

'So much the better!' Gillespie replied, and then relapsed into silence.

CHAPTER XVI - LOOKING ABOUT HIM

During the rest of that broken term Dick did little work at history: he had lost heart for Oxford, and was occupied mainly in looking out for employment, scholastic or otherwise. Employment, however, wasn't so easy to get. It never is nowadays. And Dick's case was peculiar. A certain vague suspicion always attaches to a man who has left the University, or proposes to leave it, without taking his degree. Dick found this disqualification told heavily against him. Everybody at Durham, to be sure, quite understood that Plantagenet was only going down from stress of private circumstances, the father having left his family wholly unprovided for; but elsewhere people looked askance at an applicant for work who could but give his possession of a college Scholarship as his sole credential. The Dons, of course, were more anxious that Plantagenet should stop up, to do credit to the college, he was a safe First in History, and hot favourite for the Lothian, than that he should go away and get paying work elsewhere; and in the end poor Dick began almost to despair of finding any other employment to bring in prompt cash than the hateful one at Chidding-wick, which Maud had so determinedly set her face against.

Nor was it Maud only with whom he had now to contend in that matter of the Assembly Rooms. Mary, too, was against him. As soon as Maud returned to Chiddingwick, she had made it a duty to go straight to Mary and tell her how she felt about Dick's horrid proposal. Now, Mary, at the first blush of it, had been so full of admiration for Dick's heroic resolve, 'for it was heroic, you know, Maud,' she said simply, calling her future sister-in-law for the first time by her Christian name, that she forgot at the moment the bare possibility of trying to advise Dick otherwise. But now that Maud suggested the opposite point of view to her, she saw quite clearly that Maud was right; while she herself, less accustomed to facing the facts of life, had been carried away at first sight by a specious piece of unnecessary self-sacrifice. She admired Dick all the same for it, but she recognised none the less that the heroic course was not necessarily the wisest one.

So she wrote to Dick, urging him strongly, not only for his own sake, but for hers and his family's, to keep away from Chiddingwick, save in the last extremity. She was quite ready, she declared, if he did come, to stand by every word she had said on the point when he first came to see her; but, still, Maud had convinced her that it was neither to his own interest nor his mother's and sisters' that he should turn back again now upon the upward step he had taken in going up to Oxford. She showed the letter to Maud before sending it off; and as soon as Maud had read it, the two girls, united in their love and devotion for Dick, fell on one another's necks, and kissed and cried and sobbed with all their hearts till they were perfectly happy.

All this, however, though very wise in its way, didn't make poor Dick's path any the smoother to travel. He was at his wits' end what to do. No door seemed to open for him. But fortunately Maud had commended her cause to Archie Gillespie at parting. Now, Gillespie was a practical man, with more knowledge of the world than Dick or his sweetheart, being, indeed, the son of a well-to-do Glasgow lawyer, whose business he was to join on leaving Oxford. He had discovered, therefore, the importance in this world of the eternal backstairs, as contrasted with the difficulty of effecting an entrance anywhere by the big front door or other recognised channels. So, when Sir Bernard Gillingham, that mighty man at the Foreign Office, came up on his promised visit to his son at Durham, Gillespie took good care to make the best of the occasion by getting an introduction to him from the Born Poet; and being a person of pleasant manners and graceful address, he soon succeeded in producing a most favourable impression on the mind of the diplomatist. Diplomatists are always immensely struck by a man who can speak the truth and yet be courteous. The last they exact as a sine qua non in life, but the first is a novelty to them. After awhile Gillespie mentioned to his new friend the painful case of an undergraduate of his college, Plantagenet by name, whose father had lately died under peculiar circumstances, leaving a large family totally unprovided for, and who was consequently obliged to go down without a degree and take what paying work he could find elsewhere immediately.

'Plantagenet! Let me see, that's the fellow that beat Trev for the History Scholarship, isn't it?' Sir Bernard said, musing. 'Can't be one of the Sheffield Plantagenets? No—no; for they left a round sum of money, which has never been claimed, and is still in Chancery. Extinct, I believe—extinct. Yet the name's uncommon.'

'This Plantagenet of ours claims to be something much more exalted than that,' the Born Poet answered, trying to seem unconcerned: for ever since that little affair of the recitation from Barry Neville's Collected Works, his conscience or its substitute had sorely smitten him. 'I believe he wouldn't take the other Plantagenets' money if it came to him by right: he's so firmly convinced he's a son and heir of the genuine blood royal. He never says so, of course; he's much too cute for such folly. But he lets it be seen through a veil of profound reserve he's the real Simon Pure of Plantagenets, for all that; and I fancy he considers the Queen herself a mere new-fangled Stuart, whom he probably regards as Queen of Scots only.'

'Plantagenet!' Sir Bernard went on, still in the same musing voice, hardly heeding his son. 'And a specialist in history! One would say the man was cut out for the Pipe-roll or the Record Office.'

'He knows more about the history of the Plantagenet period than any man I ever met,' Gillespie put in, striking while the iron was hot. 'If you should happen to hear of any chance at the Record Office, now, or any department like that, a recommendation from you—'

Sir Bernard snapped his fingers. 'Too late by fifty years!' he cried, with a pout of discontent—'too late by fifty years, at the very least, Mr. Gillespie! The competitive examination system has been the ruin of the country! Why, look at the sort of young men that scrape in somehow nowadays, even into the diplomatic service-some of them, I assure you, with acquired h's, which to my mind are almost worse than no Ws at all, they're so painfully obtrusive. I mean Trev for the diplomatic service; and in the good old days, before this nonsense cropped up, I should have said to the fellow at the head of the F. O. for the time being: "Look here, I say, Smith or Jones, can't you find my eldest boy a good thing off the reel in our line somewhere?" And, by Jove! sir, before the week was out, as safe as houses, I'd have seen that boy gazetted outright to a paid attachéship at Rio or Copenhagen. But what's the case nowadays? Why, ever since this wretched examination fad has come up to spoil all, my boy'll have to go in and try his luck, helter-skelter, against all the tinkers and tailors, and soldiers and sailors, and butchers and bakers, and candlestick-makers in the United Kingdom. That's what examinations have done for us. It's simply atrocious!'

Gillespie, with native tact, poured oil on the troubled waters.

'There are departments of the public service,' he said with polite vagueness, 'where birth and position no doubt enable a man to serve the State better than most of us others can serve it; and diplomacy is one of them. But, even judged by that standard, the name of Plantagenet is surely one which has done solid work in its time for the country; for the monarch, as Joseph the Second so profoundly said, is the chief of the Civil Service. As to examinations'—and he looked at Sir Bernard with a quiet smile—'men of the world like yourself know perfectly well there are still many posts of a reserved character which the head of a department holds, and must hold, in his own gift personally.'

Sir Bernard gazed hard at him and smiled a mollified smile.

'Oh, you've found that out already, have you?' he murmured dryly. 'Well, you're a very intelligent and well-informed young man: I wouldn't object to you at all for a Secretary of Legation. A secretary, as a rule, is another name for a born fool; they're put there by the F. O. on purpose to annoy one.'

And he smiled a bland smile, and nodded sagely at Gillespie. But no more was said for the moment about a post for Dick Plantagenet.

As father and son sat together at lunch, however, that morning in Edward Street, the Born Poet recurred somewhat tentatively to the intermitted subject.

'I wish, pater,' he said with assumed carelessness, 'you could manage to do something or other for that fellow Plantagenet. He's not a bad sort, though he's eccentric; and he's a real dab at history. He's been a protégé of mine in a way since he came to Durham; and though he gives himself mysterious airs on the strength of his name, and is a bit of a smug at times, still there are really points about him. He's simply wonderful on Henry the Second.'

Sir Bernard hummed and hawed, and helped himself reflectively to another devilled anchovy.

'This cook does savouries remarkably well,' he replied, with oblique regard. 'I never tasted anything better than these and his stuffed Greek olives. Such places exist, of course, but they're precious hard to get. Special aptitude for the work, and very close relationship to a Cabinet Minister, are indispensable qualifications. However, I'll bear it in mind, I'll bear it in mind for you, Trevor. I shall be dining with Sir Everard on Tuesday week, and I'll mention the matter to him.'

Whether Sir Bernard mentioned the matter to the famous Minister or not, history fails to record for us. That sort of history always goes unwritten. But it happened, at any rate, that by the end of the next week the Dean called up Gillespie after lecture one morning, and informed him privately that a letter had arrived that day from a distinguished person, inquiring particularly after Mr. Richard Plantagenet's qualifications for the post of Assistant-Decipherer to the Pipe-roll and Tally Office, with special reference to his acquaintance with legal Norman-French and mediæval Latin.

'And I was able,' the Dean added, 'to enclose in my reply a most satisfactory testimonial to your friend's knowledge of both from our two chief history lecturers.'

Gillespie thanked him warmly, but said nothing to Dick about it.

Three days later a big official envelope, inscribed in large print 'On Her Majesty's Service,' arrived at the door of Third Pair left, Back Quad, addressed to Richard Plantagenet, Esq.,.Durham College, Oxford. Dick opened it with great trepidation; this was surely a bad moment to come down upon his poor purse with a demand for income tax. But he read the contents with breathless astonishment. It was to the effect that the Right Honourable the Director of Pipe-rolls, having heard of Mr. Plantagenet as possessing a unique acquaintance with Norman-French documents, and an efficient knowledge of mediæval Latin, desired to offer him the post of Assistant Registrar and Chief Clerk in his office, an appointment directly in the Bight Honourable's own gift, and carrying with it a salary commencing at two hundred and fifty pounds a year, and rising by annual increments of ten pounds at a time to a maximum of four hundred.

To the family at Chiddingwick such an income as that was unimagined wealth beyond the dreams of avarice. Dick rushed off with the letter in hot haste to Gillespie, who received him with the quiet smile of a consummate confederate.

'The only thing about it that makes me hesitate,' Dick cried, with a strange moisture in his clear blue eyes, 'is just this, Gillespie, oughtn't the post by rights to have been put up to public competition? Mayn't I perhaps be keeping some better man out of it?'

Gillespie smiled again; he had been fully prepared beforehand for that qualm of the sensitive Plantagenet conscience.

'My dear fellow,' he said, pressing Dick's arm, 'that's not a question for you, don't you see, at all, but for the Government and the Legislature. If they choose to decide that this particular post is best filled up by private nomination, I don't think it's for the nominee to raise the first objection, especially when he's a man who must feel himself capable of doing the particular work in question at least as well as any other fellow in England is likely to do it. I'm no great believer myself in the immaculate wisdom of kings or governments, which seem to me to consist, like any other committee, of human beings; but there are some posts, I really think and believe, that can best be filled up by careful individual choice, and not by competition; and this post you're now offered seems to me just one of them. If governments always blundered on as good a man to do the work that then and there wants doing, why, I, for one, would be a deal better satisfied with them.'

So that very afternoon Dick went down to Chiddingwick to bear news to Maud and his mother of this piece of good fortune that had dropped as it seemed from the clouds upon them. For he never knew, either then or afterwards, what part that wily diplomate, Sir Bernard Gillingham, had borne in procuring the offer of the post for him. If he had known, it is probable he would have declined to accept any favour at all from the father of the man who, as he firmly believed, had helped to kill his father. Maud's triumph and delight, however, were unclouded and unbounded; this event served to show the wisdom of her pet policy; but she seemed hardly so much astonished at the news, Dick thought, as he himself had expected. This was the less to be wondered at, because, in point of fact, it was not quite so novel to her as it had been to Dick; for at that very moment Maud carried in her bosom a small square note, beginning, 'Dear Miss Plantagenet,' and signed, 'Ever yours most sincerely, Archibald Gillespie,' in which the probability of just such an offer being made before long was not obscurely hinted at. However, Maud kept that letter entirely to herself; it was not the first, or the last, she received from the same quarter.

This change of front affected all their movements. As soon as term was ended, Dick went up to London to take up the duties and emoluments of his office. But that was not all. By Gillespie's advice, Gillespie seemed to take an almost fraternal interest now in the affairs of the family, Mrs. Plantagenet and the children moved to London, too, to be with Dick in his lodgings. Gillespie thought Miss Plantagenet's musical taste so remarkable, he said, that she ought to be intown, where sound instruction could be got in singing; and he was so full of this point that Maud consented to give up her own work at Chiddingwick and take a place as daily governess in London instead, going out in the afternoon to a famous vocalist. Gillespie believed they ought all to be removed as far as possible from the blighting memory of their father's degradation; and he attached so much importance to this matter that he came down once or twice to Chiddingwick himself during the Christmas vacation, in order to see them all safely removed to Pimlico.

It was wonderful, Dick thought, what a brotherly interest that good fellow always took in all that concerned them; yet when he said so to Maud, that unconscionable young woman only blushed and looked down with a self-conscious air that was very unusual to her. But there! girls are so queer: though Gillespie had been so kind, Maud never once said a word, as one might naturally have expected, about how nice he had been to them. For his part, Dick thought her almost positively ungrateful.

CHAPTER XVII - IN SEARCH OF AN ANCESTOR

Dick's first year at the Pipe-roll was anything but a lazy one. Opulence in the shape of two hundred and fifty a year came to him with the encumbrance of plenty to do for it. He had the office routine to learn, and rolls and tallies to decipher, and endless household difficulties of his own to meet, and all the children's schooling and other arrangements to look after, It was still a struggle. But by dint of hard work and pinching, with Maud's able assistance, things came straight in the end somehow. Dick got a pupil or two in his spare time, happier men than himself, who were going up under luckier auspices to Oxford; for, though Dick put the best face upon it, still, it was a pull leaving that beloved University without a degree. However, the year wore on, as most years wear on, good, bad, or indifferent; and Mary Tudor, too, left her place at Chiddingwick Rectory, and got another one, better paid, with nice people in Westminster. She was a constant Sunday visitor at the Plantagenets' rooms; and so, in vacation, was Archie Gillespie, whose unfailing devotion to his college friend struck Dick every day as something truly remarkable. Brothers are so dense. Maud smiled at him often. If he had paid a quarter the attention to any other girl that Archie paid her, how instantly she would have perceived it! But Dick, dear Dick, never seemed to suspect that Archie could come for anything else on earth except to talk over the affairs of the family with him. And yet men consider women the inferior creatures!

Much of Dick's spare time, however, for, being a very busy man, of course he had often spare time on his hands, amounting frequently to as much as half an hour together, was spent in a curious yet congenial occupation, the laborious hunting-up of the Plantagenet pedigree. A certain insane desire to connect his family with the old Royal House of England pursued Dick through life, and made him look upon this purely useless and ornamental object as though it were a matter of the gravest practical importance. Maud felt its gravity, too, quite as much as her brother; it was an almost inevitable result, indeed, of their peculiar upbringing.

Every man has, necessarily, what the French call, well, 'the defects of his qualities'—faults which are either the correlatives or the excess of his particular virtues. Now, the Plantagenets had preserved their strong sense of self-respect and many other valuable personal characteristics under trying circumstances, by dint of this self-same family pride. It was almost necessary, therefore, that when Dick found himself in a position to prove, as he thought, the goodness of his claim to represent in our day the old Plantagenet stock, he should prosecute the research after the missing links with all the innate energy of his active nature.

Mary Tudor, indeed, whose practical common-sense was of a different order, sometimes regretted that Dick should waste so much valuable time on so unimportant an object; to her it seemed a pity that a man whose days were mainly spent in poring over dusty documents in the public service should devote a large part of his evenings as well to poring over other equally dusty documents for a personal and purely sentimental purpose.

'What good will it do you, Dick, even if you do find out you're the rightful heir to the throne of England?' she asked him more than once. 'Parliament won't repeal the Acts of Union with Scotland and Ireland, and get rid of the Settlement, to make you King and Maud and Nellie Princesses of the blood royal.'

Dick admitted that was so; but, still, her frivolity shocked him.

'It's a noble inheritance!' he said, with a touch of romance in his voice. 'Surely, Mary, you wouldn't wish me to remain insensible, like a log, to the proud distinction of so unique an ancestry! They were such men, those old Plantagenets! Look at Henry II., for example, who founded our House for most practical purposes; there was a wonderful organizer for you! And Edward I.—what a statesman! so far before his age! and the Black Prince—and Edward III.—and Henry V., what strategists! It isn't merely that they were kings, mind you; I don't care about that; since I came to know what really makes a man great, I haven't attached so much importance to the mere fact of their position. But just see what workers the old Plantagenets were in themselves, and how much they did for the building-up of England—and, indeed, of all Britain, if it comes to that, for wasn't Scotch independence itself a direct result of the national opposition to Edward Plantagenet's premature policy of unification? When I think of all those things I feel a glow of pride; I realize to myself what a grand heritage it is to be the descendant and representative of such early giants; for there were giants in those days, and no man could then be King unless he had at least a strenuous personality—oftenest, too, unless he were also a real live statesman. Our ancestors themselves knew all that very well; and when one of our line fell short of his ancestral standard, like Edward II. and Richard II., he went soon to the wall, and made way for a stronger. It's not about them I care, nor about mere puling devotees like poor Henry III.; it's my descent from men like those great early organizers, and thinkers, and rulers, who built up the administrative and judicial system we all still live under.'

When he talked like that, Maud thought it was really beautiful. She wondered how Mary could ever be insensible to the romantic charms of such old descent. But there! Mary wasn't a Plantagenet—only a mere Welsh Tudor; and though she was a dear good girl, and as sweet as they're made, how could you expect her to enter fully into the feelings of the real old family? As for Archie Gillespie, he said to Mary more than once:

'Let Dick go his own way, Miss Tudor; it gives him pleasure. He thinks some mysterious good is going to come out of it all for him and his, if he can fill in the missing links in the Plantagenet pedigree. Of course, that's pure moonshine. Still, we must always remember it was the Plantagonet pedigree that gave our Dick his first interest in English history, and so made him what he is; and anything deserves respect which could keep Edmund Plantagenet's children from degenerating, as they would have degenerated, from their father's example, without this inspiriting idea of noblesse oblige: an idea which has made Dick and Maud, I mean, Miss Plantagenet, hold their heads high through life in spite of their poverty. It can do Dick no harm now to pursue a little farther this innocent hobby; it will give him a better insight into the by-ways and alleys of early English history; and if he can really establish the Plantagenet pedigree throughout, it may serve to call attention to him as a sound historical researcher. Fortunately, he knows what evidence is; and he won't go wrong, therefore, by making heedless assumptions and incredible skips and jumps, like half our genealogists.'

So Dick persevered for fully twelve months in his eager attempt, by hook and by crook, to trace his own family up to Lionel of Clarence, upon whom Mr. Plantagenet himself had early fixed, at pure haphazard, as the special transmitter of the Plantagenet blood to the later branches of the House, himself included. The longer Dick worked at it, too, the more confident he became of ultimate success. Step by step turned out right. He had brought the thing down, he told Mary, to a moral certainty; only one link now remained to complete the entire pedigree. That's always the way, it may be mentioned parenthetically, with your doubtful genealogy; there's only one link missing, but, unfortunately, that's the link on proof of which the whole chain is dependent. And very naturally, too: for this is how the thing works out. You track your own genealogy, let us say, back to a person named Plantagenet, who lived some time in the sixteenth century, and with whom you are really and undoubtedly connected by an unbroken and traceable ancestral series. Then you track the family tree of Lionel of Clarence forward, in the opposite direction, to a real and historical Plantagenet who 'flourished,' as the books say, near the end of the fifteenth century. After that you say: 'If my ancestor, the sixteenth-century Plantagenet, turns out to be the son of Lionel's descendant in the fifteenth century, as is extremely probable, why, then, it's all made out, I'm descended direct from Lionel of Clarence; and in any case, don't you see, there's only one link missing!' Wise genealogists usually abstain on purpose from the attempt to hunt up that fatal missing link; they know right well that the safest plan is to assume identity, while efforts at proving it are frequently disastrous. But Dick was still young, and not perhaps overwise; so once he had brought down the matter to a question of a solitary missing link, he couldn't rest night or day till he had finally settled it.

One evening he returned home from the office to Maud, overflowing with a new and most important discovery.

'Well, the thing's all but proved, at last!' he cried in a triumphant voice, as he kissed her warmly; 'at least, that is to say, I've found a valuable clue that will decide the matter finally one way or the other. I've discovered a conveyance of the sixteenth century, dated 1533, here's a verbatim copy of it, which describes Thomas Plantagenet, our great-great-grandfather's grandfather, as being really the son of Giles Plantagenet, the missing-link man, who is said in it to have owned a house, and this, you will see, is the new and important point, at Framlingham, in Suffolk. He seems to have been some sort of a petty tradesman.

Where Giles first came from, we had till now no means of knowing. But after this clue, all we've got to do next is just to hunt up the local records at Framlingliam and find out that this Giles Plantagenet, already known to us, was the son of that Geoffrey Plantagenet of Richmond, in Yorkshire, whom I showed long ago to have been the last traceable descendant of Lionel of Clarence, and concerning whom Lysons says, without a shadow of authority, decissit sine prole, he died without issue.'

'It seems rather a leap, though, for those days, doesn't it,' Mary put in timidly, for she dreaded the effect of a disappointment upon Dick's nervous nature, 'from Richmond to Framlingham? I thought people rarely went then much beyond their own county.'

'That was true, no doubt, for the middle and lower classes,' Dick answered with a faint tinge of Plantagenet pride in his voice; 'but hardly even then, I should say, for people of such distinction as Geoffrey Plantagenet. Gentlemen of high rank, and members of the peerage and the Royal Family, had manors, you know, in many different counties, and moved on from one to another from time to time, or left them about by will to various sons and daughters. We mustn't judge such great folk by the common analogies of ordinary people.'

'Still, Dick,' Maud interposed, a little startled herself, 'even if Mary's objection doesn't hold good, it does seem a little odd, doesn't it, that Giles Plantagenet should be a petty tradesman at Framlingham, if he was really the son of such a man as Geoffrey, whom we know to have been a county gentleman of distinction in Yorkshire?'

'I don't think so at all,' Dick answered with a little surprise. 'In those days, you see, Maud, when there was no middle class, people went up and down easily. Attainder was so common, and loss of estates such an every-day occurrence, that the vicissitudes of families must often have been much more rapid and startling than nowadays. Moreover, it's no use arguing beforehand about a plain question of fact. It was so, or it wasn't. I shall soon find out which. The records are almost sure to be preserved at Framlingham, because it was the seat of the Howards; and I shall go down there next Bank Holiday and settle the question. After that, I'll publish the result of my search; and then nobody will ever be able to say in future we made a false pretence of being real royal Plantagenets.'

He spoke so confidently that he really frightened poor Mary. She couldn't help thinking what a terrible shock it would be to him if by any chance he should turn out after all to be mistaken, and if Giles Plantagenet should prove to be other than the son of Geoffrey.

So real did this danger appear to her, indeed, that as Bank Holiday approached, and Dick talked more and more certainly of his visit to Framling-ham, she spoke quite seriously on the matter to Maud.

'Do you know, dear,' she said, taking her friend's hand, 'if I could have got away for the day, I'd go right down to Framlingham with him, though it seems to me a dreadful waste of money for so useless a purpose.' At that, Maud's eyes flashed; poor dear Mary! she never would understand the feelings of a Plantagenet. 'What I feel is this,' Mary went on, all unheeding: 'I'm obliged to stop at home that day with the children; but I wish I could go: for if by any chance it should happen to turn out that' Dick was mistaken after all, and Giles Plantagenet wasn't the son of Geoffrey, I'm afraid the shock would quite unman him for the moment, and I hardly know what he might be tempted to do in the first keen sense of intense disappointment.'

Maud's lip curled slightly. Nursery governess as she was, the old dancing-master's daughter had all the pride of a Duchess, and why not, indeed, since she was a Princess of the blood royal?

'Oh, that wouldn't make any difference, dear,' she answered confidently. 'We are Plantagenets, don't you see? And if we don't happen to be descended from that particular man Geoffrey, we must be descended through some other member of the Plantagenet family. My poor father was sure of it; and it's always been known in Yorkshire for many generations.'

However, Mary was so urgent, and so afraid of the consequences of a sudden disappointment, for she knew Dick's nature, and loved him dearly, that at last Maud consented to accompany her brother on his projected trip, and guard him against the results of an impossible failure.

Bank Holiday came in due time, a lovely summer day; and Dick and Maud went down together by cheap train to Framlingham. The banks by the side of the rail were thick with flowers. They reached there early in the day, and Dick called upon the Rector at once, sending in his card with name and address at the Pipe-rolls. As he expected, that introduction amply sufficed him. Nor was he disappointed about the preservation of the Framlingham records. The church possessed a singularly perfect collection of baptismal and marriage entries from the beginning of the fifteenth century onward. In less than half an hour Dick was thick in their midst, turning over the dusty leaves of those worn old books with all the eagerness and enthusiasm of a born genealogist.

Maud sat with him for awhile in the gloom of that dimly-lighted chancel; but after half an hour or more of hunting page by page, her patience began to give out, and she proposed to stroll away towards the castle ruins, and return a little later to see how Dick progressed with his quest after ancestors. Dick acquiesced readily enough, and Maud went off by herself down the leafy lane that leads straight to the castle.

For some time she amused herself in the deep hollow of the moat, and waited round the great circuit of the frowning rampart. It was a splendid ruin, she thought, the finest she had seen. Then she mounted the broken wall, and looked out upon the wide plain, and admired the beautiful view of the church and village. A flag floated from the tower, as if in honour of Dick's presence. At last, as lunch-time approached, she lounged back lazily to Dick. They had brought their own bread and cheese and a few sandwiches with them, and she had picked out mentally a cool spot under the spreading chestnuts, which seemed to her the very place in which to make their impromptu picnic. So she opened the church door in very good spirits, for the fresh country air had exhilarated her like champagne after so long a spell of that dusty London; and she went straight to the chancel, where she had left poor Dick an hour before among his tattered registers.

As she drew near, a sudden terror rushed over her unexpectedly. What on earth could this mean? Dick was gazing at the books with an ashen-white face, and with eyes that fairly started out of their sockets for staring. He raised his head and looked at her. He couldn't speak for horror. With one hand he beckoned his sister mysteriously to his side; then he moistened his lips at last and pointed with one accusing finger to the entries.

'Look there, Maud,' he faltered with a painful effort; and Maud looked where he bid her.

It was a mongrel entry, half Latin, half English: 'Die 14 Junii, anno 1498, Giles, the son of Richard Plantagenet, cobbler, and of Joan, uxoris eius, huius parochiæ.'

Maud glanced at the words herself with a certain vague sense of terror.

'But perhaps,' she cried, 'after all, this Richard Plantagenet himself was of royal ancestry.'

Dick shook his head with a terrible, a despondent shake. He knew when he was beaten.

'Oh no,' he answered aloud, though he could hardly frame the words. 'I know what I say. I've found out all about this Richard Plantagenet, Maud. He was the ancestor of the other people, the false Plantagenets, don't you know, the Sheffield family who left the money. He never was a true Plantagenet in any way at all. It was only a nickname. He acted the parts of the Plantagenet kings, one after the other, in a masque or pageant, and was known from that time by pure fun as Richard Plantagenet. But that was in London; and we didn't know till now he was ever settled at Framlingham.

'And must we be descended from him, Dick?' She asked it piteously, pleadingly.

'Oh, Maud, yes, we must. There's no other way out of it. I've worked up the whole thing so thoroughly now, to my own destruction. I know all about him. His real name was Muggins; and that's our real name, too; and this book, this horrid book gives all the facts necessary to prove our descent from him; and the Sheffield people's, too, who are really our cousins.'

He said it with utter despondency. The truth was wrenched out of him. Maud clasped her white hands and looked hard at poor Dick. This disillusion was just as terrible for her as for him.

'You're quite, quite sure?' she murmured once more in a voice of pure agony.

'Yes, quite, quite sure,' Dick answered with a tremor, but with manful persistence. 'There can't be a doubt of it. I knew everything about this wretched creature before, except that he was a Framlingham man; and there are entries here in the book, you can see them for yourself, that leave no shadow of doubt anywhere about the fellow's identity. Maud, Maud, it's been all a foolish, foolish dream! We are not, we never were, real royal Plantagenets!'

Maud looked down at the ground and burst into hot tears.

'Then I'll never marry Archie,' she cried. 'Never, never, never! I'll never ask him to take a mere nobody from Chiddingwick. My pride wouldn't allow it, my pride would stand in the way, for I'm as proud as before, Dick, though I'm not a Plantagenet!'

That journey back to town was one of the most terrible things Maud had ever yet known in her poor little life. Dick leaned back disconsolate in one corner of the carriage, and she in the opposite one. Neither spoke a single word; neither needed to speak, for each knew without speech what the other was thinking of. Every now and again Dick would catch some fresh shade of expression coursing like a wave over Maud's unhappy face, and recognise in it the very idea that a moment before had been passing through his own troubled mind. It was pitiable to see them. Their whole scheme of life had suddenly and utterly broken down before them; their sense of self-respect was deeply wounded, nay, even their bare identity was all but gone, for the belief that they were in very truth descendants of the royal Plantagenets had become as it were an integral part of their personality, and woven itself intimately into all their life and thought and practice. They ceased to be themselves in ceasing to be potential princes and princesses.

For the Great Plantagenet Delusion which Edmund Plantagenet had started, and only half or a quarter believed in himself, became to his children from youth upward, and especially to Maud and Dick, a sort of family religion. It was a theory on which they based almost everything that was best and truest within them; a moral power for good, urging them always on to do credit to the great House from which they firmly and unquestioningly believed themselves to be sprung. Probably the moral impulse was there first by nature; probably, too, they inherited it, not from poor, drunken, do-nothing Edmund Plantagenet himself, through whom ostensibly they should have derived their Plantagenet character, but from that good and patient nobody, their hard-working mother. But none of these things ever occurred at all to Maud or Dick; to them it had always been a prime article of faith that noblesse oblige, and that their lives must be noble in order to come up to a preconceived Plantagenet standard of action. So the blow was a crushing one. It was as though all the ground of their being had been cut away from beneath their feet. They had fancied themselves so long the children of kings, with a moral obligation upon them to behave, well, as the children of kings are little given to behaving; and they had found out now they were mere ordinary mortals, with only the same inherent and universal reasons for right and high action as the common herd of us. It was a sad comedown—for a royal Plantagenet.

The revulsion was terrible. And Maud, who was in some ways the prouder of the two, and to whom, as to most of her sex, the extrinsic reason for holding up her head in the midst of poverty and disgrace had ever been stronger and more cogent than the intrinsic one, felt it much the more keenly. To women, the social side of things is always uppermost. They journeyed home in a constant turmoil of unrelieved wretchedness; they were not, they had never been, royal Plantagenots. Just like all the rest of the world—mere ordinary people! And they who had been sustained, under privations and shame, by the reflection that, if every man had his right, Dick would have been sitting that day on the divided throne of half these islands! Descendants, after all, of a cobbler and a dancing-master! No Black Prince at all in their lineage, no Henry, no Edward, no Richard, no Lionel! Cour-de-Lion a pale shade, Lackland himself taken away from them! And how everybody would laugh when they came to know the truth! Though that was a small matter. It was no minor thing like this, but the downfall of a faith, the ruin, of a principle, the break-up of a rule in life, that really counted!

There you have the Nemesis of every false idea, every unreal belief: when once it finally collapses, as collapse it needs must before the searching light of truth, it leaves us for awhile feeble, uncertain, rudderless. So Dick felt that afternoon; so he felt for many a weary week of reconstruction afterwards.

At last they reached home. 'T was a terrible home-coming. As they crept up the steps, poor dispossessed souls, they heard voices within—Mrs. Plantagenet's, and Gillespie's, and the children's, and Mary Tudor's.

Dick opened the door in dead silence and entered. He was pale as a ghost. Maud walked statelily behind him, scarcely able to raise her eyes to Archie Gillespie's face, but still proud at heart as ever. Dick sank down into a chair, the very picture of misery. Maud dropped into another without doing more than just stretch out one cold hand to Archie. Mrs. Plantagenet surveyed them both with a motherly glance.

'Why, Dick,' she cried, rushing up to him, 'what's the matter? Has there been a railway accident?'

Dick glanced back at her with affection half masked by dismay.

'A railway accident!' he exclaimed, with a groan. 'Oh, mother dear, I wish it had only been a railway accident! It was more like an earthquake. It's shaken Maud and me to the very foundations of our nature!' Then he looked up at her half pityingly. She wasn't a Plantagenet except by marriage; she never could quite feel as they did the sanct—And then he broke off suddenly, for he remembered with a rush that horrid, horrid truth. He blurted it out all at once: 'We are not, we never were, real royal Plantagenets!'

'I was afraid of that,' Mary Tudor said simply. 'That was just why I was so anxious dear Maud should go with you.'

Gillespie said nothing, but for the first time in public he tried to take Maud's hand for a moment in his. Maud drew it away quickly.

'No, Archie,' she said, with a sigh, making no attempt at concealment; 'I can never, never give it to you now again, for to-day I know we've always been nobodies.'

'You're what you always were to me,' Gillespie answered, in a low voice. 'It was you yourself I loved, Maud, not the imaginary honours of the Plantagenet family.'

'But I don't want to be loved so,' Maud cried, with all the bitterness of a wounded spirit. 'I don't want to be loved for myself. I don't want anyone to love me, except as a Plantagenet.'

Dick was ready, in the depth of his despair and the blackness of his revulsion, to tell out the whole truth, and spare them, as he thought, no circumstance of their degradation.

'Yes, we went to Framlingham princes and princesses, and more than that,' he said, almost proud to think whence and how far they had fallen'; 'we return from it beggars. I looked up the whole matter thoroughly, and there's no room for hope left, no possibility of error. The father of Giles Plantagenet, from whom we're all descended, most fatally descended, was one Richard, called Plantagenet, but really Muggins, a cobbler at Framlingham; the same man, you know, Mary, that I told you about the other day. In short, we're just cousins of the other Plantagenets, the false Plantagenets, the Sheffield Plantagenets, the people who left the money.'

He fired it off at them with explosive energy. Mary gave a little start.

'But surely in that case, Dick,' she cried, 'you must be entitled to their fortune! You told me one day it was left by will to the descendants and heirs-male of Richard Muggins, alias Plantagenet, whose second son George was the ancestor and founder of the Sheffield family.'

'So he was,' Dick answered dolefully, without a light in his eye. 'But, you see, I didn't then know, or suspect, or even think possible, what I now find to be the truth, the horrid, hateful truth, that our ancestor, Giles Plantagenet, whom I took to be the son of Geoffrey, the descendant of Lionel, Duke of Clarence, was in reality nothing more than the eldest son of this wretched man Richard Muggins; and the elder brother of George Muggins, alias Plantagenet, who was ancestor of the Sheffield people who left the money.'

'But if so,' Gillespie put in, 'then you must be the heirs of the Plantagenets who left the money, and must be entitled, as I understand, to something like a hundred and fifty or a hundred and sixty thousand pounds sterling!'

'Undoubtedly,' Dick answered in a tone of settled melancholy. .

Gillespie positively laughed, in spite of himself, though Maud looked up at him through her tears, and murmured:

'Oh, Archie, how can you?

'Why, my dear follow,' he said, taking Dick's arm, 'are you really quite sure it's so? Are you perfectly certain you've good legal proof of the identity of this man Giles with your own earliest ancestor, and of the descent of your family from the forefather of the Sheffield people?'

'I'm sorry to say,' Dick answered with profound dejection, 'there can't be a doubt left of it. It's too horribly certain. Hunting up these things is my trade, and I ought to know. I've made every link in the chain as certain as certainty. I have a positive entry for every step in the pedigree, not doubtful entries, unfortunately, but such conclusive entries as leave the personality of each person beyond the reach of suspicion. Oh, it's a very bad business, a terrible business!' And he flung his arms on the table, and leaned over it himself, the very picture of mute misery.

'Then you believe the money's yours?' Gillespie persisted, half incredulous.

'Believe it!' Dick answered. 'I don't believe it; I know it is, the wretched stuff! There's no dodging plain facts. I can't get out of it, anyhow.'

'Did you realize that this money would be yours when you saw the entries at Framlingham?' Gillespie inquired, hardly certain how to treat such incredible behaviour.

'I didn't think of it just at once,' Dick answered with profound despair in his voice; 'but it occurred to me in the train, and I thought how terrible it would be to confess it before the whole world by claiming the wretched money. Though it might perhaps be some consolation, after all, to poor mother.'

'And you, Maud?' Gillespie inquired, turning round to his sweetheart, and with difficulty repressing a smile. 'Did you think at all of it?'

'Well, I knew if we were really only false Plantagenets, like the Sheffield people,' Maud answered bravely through the tears that struggled hard to fall, 'we should probably in the end come into their money. But oh, Archie, it isn't the money Dick and I would care for. Let them take back their wealth, let them take it, if they will! But give us once more our own Plantagenet ancestry!'

Gillespie drew Mary aside for a moment.

'Say nothing to them about it for the present,' he whispered in her ear. 'Let the first keen agony of their regret pass over. I can understand their feeling. This myth had worn itself into the very warp and woof of their natures. It was their one great inheritance. The awakening is a terrible shock to them. All they thought themselves once, all they practically were for so many years together, they have suddenly ceased to be. This grief and despair must wear itself out. For the present we mustn't even inquire of them about the money.'

And indeed it was a week or two before Dick could muster up heart to go with Archie Gillespie to a lawyer about the matter. When he did, however, he had all the details of the genealogy, all the proofs of that crushing identification he had longed to avoid, so fully at his finger-ends, that the solicitor whom he consulted, and to whom he showed copies of the various documents in the case, hadn't a moment's doubt as to the result of his application. 'I suppose this will be a long job, though,' Gillespie suggested, 'and may want a lot of money, to prosecute it to its end?

It'll have to be taken for an indefinite time into Chancery, won't it?'

'Not at all,' the solicitor answered. 'It's very plain sailing. We can get it through at once. There's no hitch in the evidence. You see, it isn't as if there were any opposition to the claim, any other descendants. There are none, and by the very nature of the case there can't be any. Mr. Plantagenet has anticipated and accounted for every possible objection. The thing is as clear as mud. His official experience has enabled him to avoid all the manifold pitfalls of amateur genealogists. I never saw an inheritance that went so far back made more absolutely certain.'

Poor Dick's heart sank within him. He knew it himself already; but still, he had cherished throughout some vague shadow of a hope that the lawyer might discover some faint flaw in the evidence which, as he considered, had disinherited him. There was nothing for it now but to pocket at once the Plantagenet pride and the Plantagenet thousands, to descend from his lofty pedestal and be even as the rest of us are, except for the fortune. He turned to Gillespie with a sigh.

'I was afraid of this,' he said. 'I expected that answer. Well, well, it'll make my dear mother happy; and it'll at least enable me to go back again to Oxford.'

That last consideration was indeed in Maud's eyes the one saving grace of an otherwise hopeless and intolerable situation. Gradually, bit by bit, though it was a very hard struggle, they reconciled themselves to their altered position. The case was prepared, and, as their lawyer had anticipated, went straight through the courts with little or no difficulty, thanks to Dick's admirable working up of all the details of the pedigree. By the time eight months were out, Dick had come into the inheritance of 'the Plantagenets who left the money,' and was even beginning to feel more reconciled in his heart to the course of events which had robbed him so ruthlessly of his fancied dignity, but considerably added to his solid comfort.

Before Dick returned to Oxford, however, to finish his sadly interrupted University career, he had arranged with Mary that as soon as he took his degree they two should marry. As for poor Maud, woman that she was, the loss of that royal ancestry that had never been hers seemed to weigh upon her even more than it weighed upon her brother. The one point that consoled her under this crushing blow was the fact that Archie, for whose sake she had minded it most at first, appeared to care very little indeed whether the earliest traceable ancestor of the girl he loved had been a royal Plantagenet or a shoemaking Muggins. It was herself he wanted, he said with provoking persistence, not her great-great-great grandfathers. Maud could hardly understand such a feeling herself; for when Archie first took a fancy to her, she was sure it must have been her name and her distinguished pedigree that led an Oxford man and a gentleman, with means and position, to see her real good points through the poor dress and pale face of the country dancing-master's daughter.

Still, if Archie thought otherwise—Well, as things had turned out, she was really glad; though, to be sure, she always felt in her heart he didn't attach quite enough importance to the pure Plantagenet pedigree that never was theirs, but that somehow ought to have been. However, with her share of that hateful Sheffield money she was now a lady, she said—Archie strenuously denied she could ever have been anything else, though Maud shook her head sadly—and when Archie one day showed her the photograph of a very pretty place among the Campsie Fells which his father had just bought for him, 'in case of contingencies,' and asked her whether she fancied she could ever be happy there, Maud rose with tears in her eyes and laid her hand in his, and answered earnestly:

'With you, dearest Archie, I'm sure I could be happy, my life long, anywhere.'

And from that day forth she never spoke to him again of the vanished glories of the Plantagenet pedigree.

Perhaps it was as well they had believed in it once. That strange myth had kept them safe from sinking in the quicksands when the danger was greatest. It had enabled them to endure, and outlive with honour, much painful humiliation. It had been an influence for good in moulding their characters. But its work was done now, and 'twas best it should go.

Slowly Dick and Maud began to realize that themselves. And the traces it left upon them, after the first poignant sense of loss and shame had worn off, were all for the bettering of their moral natures.

Grant Allen – A Short Biography

Charles Grant Blairfindie Allen was born on February 24th, 1848 at Alwington, near Kingston, Canada West (now part of Ontario). He was the second son of the Rev. Joseph Antisell Allen, a Protestant minister from Dublin, Ireland and Catharine Ann Grant, the daughter of the fifth Baron of Longueuil.

Grant was educated at home until he was thirteen at which time the family moved, initially to the United States, then France and finally settling in the United Kingdom.

Whilst growing up the family background was obviously religious but Grant developed his own views on life and the world and turned to agnosticism and socialism.

He was educated at King Edward's School in Birmingham and Merton College in Oxford. After graduating, Grant studied in France and also taught at Brighton College. By 1870, still only in his mid-twenties, he became a professor at Queen's College, a black college in Jamaica.

Whilst in Jamaica Grant met and married his first wife Ellen Jerrard in 1873 and they produced a son five years later; Jerrard Grant Allen, who grew up to become a theatrical agent/manager.

In 1876 Grant and his family left Jamaica to return to England with both the talent and ambition to become a writer.

He quickly turned to writing essays, gaining a reputation for his work on science and literary works. An early article, 'Note-Deafness' a description of what is now called amusia, was published in 1878 in the learned journal Mind and was cited approvingly by Oliver Sacks very recently.

From essays in magazines and journals he now turned to books, initially on scientific subjects. These include Physiological Æsthetics 1877 and Flowers and Their Pedigrees 1886.

His first major influence was associationist psychology, as then expounded by Alexander Bain and Herbert Spencer, the latter is often considered the most important individual in the transition from associationist psychology to Darwinian functionalism. In Grant's many articles on flowers and perception in insects, Darwinian arguments now replaced the old Spencerian terms.

On a personal level, a long friendship that started when Grant met Herbert Spencer on his return from Jamaica, turned eventually to one of unease over its long course. Grant was to write a critical and revealing biographical article on Spencer that was published after Spencer was dead.

In the early 1880's Grant began to assist Sir W. W. Hunter in his Gazeteer of India. It is at this time that Grant now turned his full attention away from the factual and towards the world of imagination and fiction.

Between this shift to fiction in 1884 and his death fifteen years later Grant was to write about 30 novels.

Many were adventure novels which were very common in the late Victorian period as writers turned their literary talents to the voracious appetites of the weekly or monthly serial magazines.

Some however were to cause quite a stir. For instance in 1895 Grant took the subject of children born out of wedlock as his subject matter. The result was The Woman Who Did, that suggested, indeed pushed, for its time, certain quite startling views on marriage and related areas. In keeping with his then glowing reputation it became a bestseller despite it being seemingly at odds with society's unease at its provocative subject matter.

Interestingly Grant wrote novels under female pseudonyms. One of these was the short novel The Type-writer Girl, which he wrote under the name Olive Pratt Rayner.

Another work, The Evolution of the Idea of God 1897, propounding a theory of religion on heterodox lines, has the disadvantage of endeavoring to explain everything by one theory. This "ghost theory" was often seen as a derivative of Herbert Spencer's theory. However, at the time, it was well known and brief references to it can be found in a review by Marcel Mauss, Durkheim's nephew, in the articles of William James and in the works of Sigmund Freud. The young G. K. Chesterton wrote on what he considered the flawed premise of the idea, arguing that the idea of God preceded human mythologies, rather than developing from them. Chesterton said of Grant Allen's book on the evolution of the idea of God "it would be much more interesting if God wrote a book on the evolution of the idea of Grant Allen".

From this and other instances, it can be seen that his work was in debate and whether agreed with or not could always ensure a lively discussion.

Grant also helped to pioneer science fiction, with the 1895 novel The British Barbarians. This book, was published at about the same time as H. G. Wells was to publish The Time Machine. The plots are quite different but both describe time travel. A few years later his short story The Thames Valley Catastrophe (published 1901 in The Strand magazine) describes the destruction of London by a massive volcanic eruption. Whilst the premise now may seem outlandish, at the time genuine panic and concern set in as, like his contemporary, Jules Verne, much of great science fiction writing is rooted in a plausibility that is set out very convincingly.

In detective fiction too his works include female detectives, very much an innovation in the young genre and his gentleman rogue, Colonel Clay, is seen as a forerunner to other, perhaps more famous characters, by other later writers.

In 1881 he had settled at Dorking, where he took great delight in botanical walks in the woods and sandy heaths. He never enjoyed particularly good health and so almost every winter he would depart for milder climes, to winter in the south of Europe, usually at Antibes, though occasionally as far as Algiers and Egypt.

In 1892 he bought land almost on the summit of Hind Head, and built himself a charming cottage which he called the Croft. Here he found that it was possible to endure the vagaries of the English winter and in landscape more beautiful and wilder than at Dorking and that his long scientific training could better appreciate.

His growing re-discovery and interest in art in the later part of his life allowed him to blend together literature, art and history in a series of guide books on Paris, Florence, Venice, and the cities of Belgium.

On October 25th 1899 Grant Allen died at his home in Hindhead, Haslemere, Surrey, England. He died just before finishing Hilda Wade. The novel's final episode, which he dictated to his friend, doctor and neighbour Sir Arthur Conan Doyle from his bed appeared under the appropriate title, The Episode of the Dead Man Who Spoke in the Strand Magazine in 1900.

Grant Allen is rarely heard of today, although an occasional short story can be heard on the radio or reprinted among magazine enthusiasts but in his time he did much to entertain the masses and push several genres along a richer journey they are still proceeding on today.

Grant Allen – A Concise Bibliography

Physiological Æsthetics. 1877
The Colour-Sense: Its Origin and Development. 1879
Evolutionist at Large. 1881
Vignettes from Nature. 1881
The Colours of Flowers. 1882
Colin Clout's Calendar. 1883
Flowers and Their Pedigrees. 1883
Philistia. 1884
Strange Stories. Short Stories. 1884
Babylon. A novel in 3 volumes. 1885
For Mamie's Sake. 1886
In All Shades. 1886

The Beckoning Hand & Other Stories. 1887
This Mortal Coil: A Novel. 1888
Force and Energy. 1888
The Devil's Die. 1888
The White Man's Foot. 1888
Falling in Love. 1889
The Tents of Shem. 1889
Wednesday the Tenth. 1890
The Great Taboo. 1890
Dumaresq's Daughter. 1891
What's Bred in the Bone. 1891
The Duchess of Powysland. 1892
The Scallywag. 1893
Michael's Crag. 1893
The Lower Slopes. 1894
Post-Prandial Philosophy. 1894
The British Barbarians. 1895
At Market Value. 1895
The Story of the Plants. 1895
The Desire of the Eyes. 1895
The Woman Who Did. 1895
The Jaws of Death. 1896
A Bride from the Desert. 1896
Under Sealed Orders. 1896
Moorland Idylls. 1896
An African Millionaire. Colonel Clay's novel. 1897
The Evolution of the Idea of God. 1897
Paris. 1897
The Type-writer Girl. (as Olive Pratt Rayner) 1897
Tom, Unlimited. (as Martin Leach Warborough) 1897
Flashlights on Nature. 1898
The Incidental Bishop. 1898
Venice. 1898
The European Tour. 1899
A Splendid Sin. 1899
Miss Cayley's Adventures. 1899
Twelve Tales: With a Headpiece, a Tailpiece, and an Intermezzo. 1899
Hilda Wade (finished by Arthur Conan Doyle). 1900
Linnet. 1900
The Backslider. 1901
Sir Theodore's Guest & Other Stories. 1902
Evolution in Italian Art. 1908
The Hand of God. 1909
The Plants. 1909

Short Stories
The Empress of Andorra. 1878
My New Year Among the Mummies. 1878
Lucretia. 1879
My Circular Tour. 1880

A Ballade of Evolution. 1880
Ram Das of Cawnpore. 1880
The Chinese Play at the Haymarket. 1880
The Senior Proctor's Wooing. 1881
Pausodyne. 1881
Caribbean Twelve Per Cents. 1882
An Episode in High Life. 1882
Mr Chung. 1882
Isadine and I. 1883
The Backsider. 1883
The Reverend John Creedy. 1883
The Foundering of the Fortuna. 1883
The Third Time
The Gold Wulfric
My Uncle's Will. 1884
Carvalho. 1884
The Mysterious Occurence in Piccadilly. 1884
Dr Greatex's Engagement. 1884
Hugh Portledown's Return from Normandy. 1884
The Child of Phalanstery. 1884
The Curate of Churnside. 1884
John Cann's Treasure. 1884
Olga Davidoff's Husband. 1884
The Search Party's Find. 1885
The Two Carnegie's. 1885
Professor Milliter's Dilemma. 1885
In Strict Confidence. 1885
The Beckoning Hand. 1885
The Third Time. 1886
Harry's Inheritance. 1886
The Gold Wulfric. 1886
Mr Pierpoint's Repentance. 1886
Claude Tyack's Ordeal. 1887
Leonard's Recovery. 1887
A Social Difficulty. 1887
Dr Palliser's Patient. 1888
My Christmas Eve at Marzin. 1888
The Sultan's Sister. 1888
His First Crime. 1889
The Mayfield Mystery. 1889
Andre Canivet's Curse. 1890
Old Margaret. 1890
My One Gorilla. 1890
Dick Prothero's Luck. 1890
A Deadly Dilemna. 1891
Jerry Stokes. 1891
Selwyn Utterton's Nemesis. 1891
General Passavant's Will. 1891
The Briefless Barrister. 1891
Melissa's Tour. 1891
Karen – A Canadian Romance. 1891

The Prisoner of Assiout. 1891
The Abbe's Repentance. 1891
Masie Bowman's Fate. 1891
Naomi's Christmas Eves. 1891
That Friend of Sylvia's. 1892
The Conscientious Burglar. 1892
The Minor Poet. 1892
The Governor's Story. 1892
The Pot Boiler. 1892
The Great Ruby. 1892
Ewen Murray's Swim. 1892
Ivan Greet's Masterpiece. 1892
Pallinghurst Barrow. 1892
Langalula. 1893
The Assasin's Knife. 1893
The Artist and the Penny-a-Liner. 1893
A Casual Conversation. 1893
How To Succeed in Literature. 1893
Torrigiano. 1893
A Modern Sibyl: A Florentine Sketch. 1893
Nemesis Wins. 1894
Cecca's Lover. 1894
A Self Respecting Servant. 1894
Passiflora Sanguinea. 1894
An Excellent Match. 1894
Major Kinfaun's Marriage. 1894
Grateful Joe. 1894
An Idyll of the Ice. 1894
Criss Cross Love. 1894
Poor Little Soul. 1894
Amour de Voyage. 1894
The Dynamiter's Sweetheart. 1894
A Triumph of Civilisation. 1894
Dr Wardroper's Lie. 1894
The Miraclous Explorer. 1894
Leon and Leonie. 1895
A Comic Emotion. 1895
Joe's Rascality. 1895
Evelyn Moore's Poet. 1895
Frasine's First Communion. 1895
TheDead Man Speaks. 1895
A Study From the Nude. 1895
Cecca's Choice. 1895
The Desire of the Eyes. 1895
The Making of a Poet. 1895
The Man From Cumbrae. 1895
Fogo Skerries. 1895
The Great Californian Heiress. 1895
Cap'n Tom Woolley. 1895
The Girl at the Fair. 1895
Love's Old Dream. 1895

A Modern Pygmalion. 1895
A Bride From the Desert. 1895
The Practical Test. 1896
A Confidential Communication. 1896
The Great Temperance Preacher. 1896
A Day on the River. 1896
The Episode of the Mexican Seer. 1896
A Midsummer Episode. 1896
The Episode of the Diamond Links. 1896
Omar at Marlow. 1896
A Mere Matter of Standpoint. 1896
Fair Exchange. 1896
The Cowardly Dynamiter. 1896
The Episode of the Old Master. 1896
The Episode of the Tyrolean Castle. 1896
Janet's Nemesis. 1896
Entirely Accidental. 1896
The Episode of the Drawn Game. 1896
Wolverden Tower. 1896
The Episode of the German Professor. 1896
The Episode of the Arrest of the Colonel. 1896
The Episode of the Seldom Gold Mine. 1897
The Camisard's Bride. 1897
The Episode of the Japanned Dispatch Box. 1897
Llanfihangel Skerries. 1897
The Episode of the Game of Poker. 1897
The Episode of the Bertillon Method. 1897
A Lady of Florence. 1897
The Episode of the Old Bailey. 1897
A British Verdict. 1897
A Domestic Tragedy. 1897
A College Charm. 1897
A Freak of Memory. 1897
The Judge's Cross. 1897
The Thames Valley Catastrophe. 1897
The Great Oriental Seer. 1897
The Adventures of the Cantankerous Old Lady. 1898
The Adventure of the Supercilious Attache. 1898
The Pirate of Cliveden Reach. 1898
The Adventure of the Amateur Commission. 1898.
The Adventure of the Impromptu Mountaineer. 1898
Joe's Wife. 1898
The Adventure of the Urbane Old Gentleman. 1898
The Adventure of the Unobtrusive Oasis. 1898
The Adventure of the Pea Green Patrician. 1898
Isenberg's Regiment. 1898
The Adventure of the Magnificent Maharajah. 1898
A Woman's Hand: A Story. 1898
The Adventure of the Cross Eyed QC. 1898
The Christmas Eve Concert. 1898
The Adventure of the Oriental Attendant. 1899

Joseph's Dream. 1899
The Adventure of the Unprofessional Detective. 1899
Hobbling Mary. 1899
The Episode of the Patient Who Disappointed Her Doctor. 1899
The Episode of the Gentleman Who Had Failed For Everything. 1899
The Episode of the Wife Who Did Her Duty. 1899
The Episode of the Man Who Would Not Commit Suicide. 1899
A Regrettable Error. 1899
Peace-At-Any-Price Bill. 1899
The Episode of the Letter with a Basingstoke Post-Mark. 1899
The Episode of the Stone That Looked About It. 1899
His Ways Inscrutable. 1899
The Episode of the European With A Kaffir Heart. 1899
The Episode of the Lady Who Was Very Exclusive. 1899
The Episode of the Guide Who Knew the Country. 1899
Luigi and the Salvationist. 1899.
A Christmas Adventure. 1899.
The Episode of the Officer Who Understood Perfectly. 1900
Meriel Stanley, Poacher. 1900
The Episode of the Dead Man Who Spoke. 1900
A Question of Colour. 1900
Fra Benedett's Medal: A Story. 1900
The Temple of Fate: A Fable. 1900
The Way to Keronan. 1902
Lucy Lockett. 1902
Spencerian. 1904

Articles

1878. Hellas and Civilization, Gentleman's Magazine, Vol. CCXLIII
1878. Nation-making: A Theory of National Characters, Gentleman's Magazine, Vol. CCXLIII
1878. The Origin of Fruits, in Popular Science Monthly Volume 13
1879. Why Do We Eat our Dinner? in Popular Science Monthly Volume 14
1879. A Problem in Human Evolution, in Popular Science Monthly Volume
1879. Pleased with a Feather, in Popular Science Monthly Volume 15
1880. Why Keep India? The Contemporary Review, Vol. XXXVIII
1880. The Growth of Sculpture, The Cornhill Magazine, Vol. XLII
1880. The English Chronicle, Gentleman's Magazine, Vol. CCXLV
1880. The Venerable Bede, Gentleman's Magazine, Vol. CCXLIX
1880. The Dog's Universe, Gentleman's Magazine, Vol. CCXLIX
1880. Evolution and Geological Time, Gentleman's Magazine, Vol. CCXLIX
1880. Geology and History, in Popular Science Monthly Volume 17
1880. Aesthetic Feeling in Birds, in Popular Science Monthly Volume 17
1880. Aesthetic Evolution in Man, in Popular Science Monthly Volume 18
1881. The Story of Wulfgeat, Gentleman's Magazine, Vol. CCLI
1882. An English Shire, Gentleman's Magazine, Vol. CCLII
1882. The Welsh in the West Country, Gentleman's Magazine, Vol. CCLIII
1882. The Colours of Flowers, The Cornhill Magazine, Vol. XLV
1882. An English Weed, The Cornhill Magazine, Vol. XLV
1882. Sir Charles Lyell, in Popular Science Monthly Volume 20
1882. Hyacinth-Bulbs, in Popular Science Monthly Volume 20

1882. Who was Primitive Man? in Popular Science Monthly Volume 22

1883. The Pedigree of Wheat, in Popular Science Monthly Volume 22

1883. From Buttercups to Monk's-Hood, in Popular Science Monthly Volume 23

1883. Honeysuckle, Gentleman's Magazine, Vol. CCLV

1884. The Garden Snail, Gentleman's Magazine, Vol. CCLVI

1884. Our Debt to Insects, Gentleman's Magazine, Vol. CCLVI

1884. Idiosyncrasy, in Popular Science Monthly Volume 24

1884. The Ancestry of Birds, in Popular Science Monthly Volume 24

1884. The Milk in the Cocoa-Nut, in Popular Science Monthly Volume 25

1884. Our Debt to Insects, in Popular Science Monthly Volume 25

1884. Hickory-Nuts and Butternuts, in Popular Science Monthly Volume 25

1884. Queer Flowers, in Popular Science Monthly Volume 26

1885. Food and Feeding, in Popular Science Monthly Volume 26

1885. Concerning Clover, in Popular Science Monthly Volume 28

1886. A Thinking Machine, Gentleman's Magazine, Vol. CCLX

1886. Fish Out of Water, in Popular Science Monthly Volume 28

1886. A Thinking Machine, in Popular Science Monthly Volume 28

1886. Thistles, in Popular Science Monthly Volume 30, November 1886

1887. A Mount Washington Sandwort, in Popular Science Monthly Volume 30

1887. Among the Thousand Islands, in Popular Science Monthly Volume 31

1887. The Progress of Science from 1836 to 1886, in Popular Science Monthly Volume 31

1887. American Cinque-Foils, in Popular Science Monthly Volume 32

1888. Gourds and Bottles, in Popular Science Monthly Volume 33

1888. A Living Mystery, in Popular Science Monthly Volume 33

1888. Evolving the Camel, in Popular Science Monthly Volume 34

1889. From Africa, Gentleman's Magazine, Vol. CCLXVII

1889. Genius and Talent, in Popular Science Monthly Volume 34

1889. Plain Words on the Woman Question, in Popular Science Monthly Volume 36

1890. The Girl of the Future, Universal Review, Vol. VII.

1891. Democracy and Diamonds, The Contemporary Review, Vol. LIX

1892. A Desert Fruit, in Popular Science Monthly Volume 41

1893. Ghost Worship and Tree Worship I, in Popular Science Monthly Volume 42

1893. Ghost Worship and Tree Worship II, in Popular Science Monthly Volume 42

1897. Spencer and Darwin, in Popular Science Monthly Volume 50

1898. The Romance of Race, in Popular Science Monthly Volume 53

1898. The Season of the Year, in Popular Science Monthly Volume 54

Poetry

Grant Allen wrote various poems published in many magazines etc. We have not listed them here but hope to record some of them in the future.